Midnight Companion

Kit Barrie

Midnight Companion: An MM retelling of The Legend of Sleepy Hollow

First edition

This is a work of fiction. Names, characters, places, and incidents are either the product of the author's imagination or are used fictitiously. Any resemblance to actual persons living or dead, business establishments, events, or locales is entirely coincidental. The narrative does contain direct quotes and paraphrasing from *The Legend of Sleepy Hollow* by Washington Irving, which is in the public domain. All art is used with a paid creative-commons license, and individual artist attribution is not required.

Cover Art by Kit Barrie

Artwork from The Noun Project, DepositPhotos, and Canva

ISBN Ebook: 979-8-9875574-6-4

ISBN Paperback: 979-8-9875574-7-1

Contents

Chapter One

I have always loved ghost stories. There is something about the New World that inspires such tales. Different languages and cultures thriving together in a wild, unexplored land tend to open one's imagination. I have never considered myself to be weak-minded or prone to flights of fancy, however. I grew up in the city, with religious parents and formal schooling, and I was every inch the scholar my parents wanted me to be. It is with that advisory that I, Ichabod Crane, set my quill to paper to tell my own ghost story, though one that is entirely factual rather than simply a tale to thrill the mind. I admit that it hardly seems to have any bearing on reality, and, indeed, I would not believe it myself had I not experienced it, for it is a tale too fantastical for most minds to comprehend. But I assure you that every word of it is true. Henceforth, I commend to paper the story of Sleepy Hollow in 1790 and 1791, as I experienced it.

My arrival in Sleepy Hollow had come as a surprise to all, including myself. My boyhood had been spent in the settlements of Connecticut, where I was raised on a strict diet of religion while feasting on legends and folklore with an almost apostolic appetite. I was not a boisterous child. My family was one of reservation and respect. We were not wealthy, but I was able to attend school for several years and showed an aptitude for learning. My parents encouraged my education, for it was easier to be a man of business with a good head on one's shoulders. In addition to math and science, I also learned history and literature, and I studied piano and singing, becoming quite the celebrated soprano in our local church in my youth.

My mother passed away when I was a lad of nine or ten, from childbed fever, and what would have been my younger sister, Nina, followed her to the grave. That left me in the charge of my father. He was a stern man, a man of business, for whom there was only one right answer and no excuses to be made. He had been a strict believer in the good book, until my mother left this earth. Then he seemed to lose his passion only for the will of God, finding renewed vigor at the bottom of a bottle. When drunk, he often went on zealous rants, forcing me to my knees to pray with him on the hard wood floor until I could hardly stand again. When I was able to finally escape from these long sessions of religious fervor, I retreated into reading and study. My rather prominent nose was quite often in a book. There were not very many available, even in our larger town, so every new book that I found was a rare and unexpected treat.

The time arrived when I had to decide what my path in life would be. The idea was presented of my becoming a traveling country schoolmaster. This seemed as good a career choice as any with my desire to see the world, as well as to escape my father's rigorous bouts of religion. I was trained in all manner of schoolmastery, and then I was dispatched to Westchester County in New York.

I had several short postings in various communities, finding small farming towns and outposts that needed instruction, but these were fickle, depending on the season and the desire of the inhabitants to withstand my presence. As such, I made my way along the Hudson and its various villages, carrying my meager belongings on my back.

In 1789, in the Greenburgh village of Tarry Town, I found an eager audience of young minds. I settled there for the winter and into the early spring of 1790. Indeed, I might have been happy to remain in that town for a long time to come, but the populations of such places are never as robust as the need, and I felt that it was drawing time for me to move on until a new generation of minds was ready for instruction. Upon asking the kindly family with whom I had been lodging what the nearest village to the north was, the look exchanged between the members was as if I might have asked where to find the lair of the Medusa, such was their horror and concern.

"There is nothing to the north," said Van Houten, shaking his head so vehemently that his bushy, black beard shook like a berry thicket in a windstorm.

"Surely there must be," I countered. "There is still part of Hudson left to travel, and much was settled before the war."

Another exchange happened between the Van Houtens. "Beyond Tarry Town is a cursed place," said good Madam Van Houten, a stout and dour matron whom I would have thought beyond such fancies. "No one who ventures into the glen returns."

That was not the answer I had been expecting. "How many have ventured in recent times?" I asked.

"None from our area," was the answer from Van Houten with a great snort. "Not since the end of the war, at least."

"But there is a town in the glen?" I asked.

"Yes," Van Houten said. "A single village, by the name of Sleepy Hollow."

The name was unfamiliar to me, though it evoked a calm and peaceful reverie in my mind. "Then I shall travel to Sleepy Hollow," I declared.

Both of the Van Houtens made a gesture in front of themselves like a priest drawing the sign of the cross. "Do not go," Madam Van Houten said. "For the sake of your blessed mother and father, venture no further than our town, especially as the harvest draws near."

That was probably the thing that drove my determination on like a team of charging horses, for while I was a quiet and reserved man, the desire to defy my father or any person of such authority was still strong in my breast. I was now more sure than ever that my time in Tarry Town was ending and that I would set out for Sleepy Hollow within a fortnight.

The morning of my departure, the townsfolk were as somber as a funeral procession, watching me make my way to the edge of the town through half-shaded windows and cracked doors. Before me stretched a swath of dark trees, and the dimly lit forest path almost gave me pause. But I was bound and determined not to show reluctance after my declaration that I was indeed moving on from Tarry Town, so I lifted my head high, shouldered my pack, and stepped out of the gates. A few dozen more paces, and I was at the edge of the forest. I could feel all eyes on my back, and I turned, lifting my hand in a farewell gesture to the town that had been so kind to me, before I stepped inside the line of trees.

The dimness was not as absolute as I had thought, the woods pleasant. The sun shone through the leaves, dappling my skin and the dirt road in front of me. It looked to be fairly worn from wagon wheels, and a few well-used paths branched off to the east at intervals. But the further north I walked, the more roughshod it became. More than once I caught my foot on a loose stone or hidden root; but despite my lankiness, I managed to keep myself upright until the path disappeared completely.

One moment there was a trail under my feet, and another step later, it was gone, as if an artist had drawn a line across a piece of paper. I turned back to see the path behind me. I was about to head into wild territory. For some reason, my heart picked up in my chest at that. I turned to look into the trees ahead of me again. It seemed a little darker here, with thicker overhang, so less of the late morning sunshine shown through, but it looked no different than the rest of the forest. I felt a little silly for suddenly feeling fear over something as simple as trees and a road ending. If I were to turn back now and return to Tarry Town, I felt I might not be able to live with the shame. So I lifted my chin and continued ahead.

The trees grew denser, the light dimmer, for a bit, and I became a little nervous that I might lose my way, but my steps remained confident. I was glad to be in these woods during the daytime. For while my upbringing had been filled with religion, that did not preclude me from all manner of superstitions and beliefs in the supernatural, gleaned from my many years of reading and talking with the various inhabitants of my hometown during my childhood. One does not usually see anything more frightening or unexpected than an errant rat in the city. Perhaps a corpse washing up on the river bank once in a great while, or some poor soul beaten to death in a dark street, but ghosts and goblins were the stuffs of country folk and their bucolic lives, not those of city-dwellers.

I was ruminating on this before I caught a glimpse of brightness through the trunks. I pressed on toward it, my steps picking up a little until I reached the very edge of the tree line. The world I stepped into was beautiful. A sea of golden grain and brightly colored garden plots lay before me on one side, and a field of gorgeously waving corn stalks on the other, with several quaint, Dutch-inspired houses scattered about, bright reds and whites as perfect as any painting. The grass beneath my feet was the brightest green, the sky a most generous shade of blue, the clouds bright and silvery. Very far over the hills on every side, I could see the forest, stretched out like a dark sea around this stunning hamlet of color. My feet gave an involuntary little hop as I strode out of the coolness of the woods and into the early afternoon sunlight.

A little path began to form under my feet again as I walked toward the town that I assumed must be Sleepy Hollow. I followed it, and it gradually became more rutted and wagon-worn. The corn to my right rustled, and I jumped as a man emerged from the field onto the road. His face was shielded by the sun, and he carried a sharp-looking sickle over his shoulder. When he saw me, he stopped dead in his tracks, mouth agape. I stared back at him before lifting my hand in salutation. "Hello. I am Ichabod Crane, the traveling schoolmaster for this area. Might this glen be the village of Sleepy Hollow?"

The man continued to stare, so much so that I wondered if perhaps he was deaf, before he pulled his straw hat from his head to squint at me. "Ah, sure is, good master. Ichabod Crane, you say?"

"Yes, sir," I said, giving a polite bow.

He scratched his bristly chin thoughtfully with his thumb. "Traveling schoolmaster. It has been a while since we've had one of those."

"Do you have need of one then?" I asked, and his face broke into a wide grin.

"We do, we do. Welcome, Master Crane! Ezra Brouwer. Might you be heading into the square?"

"Wherever I may speak with the leader of the town," I said.

"That would be Baltus Van Tassel," Ezra said, scratching at his stubble again. "He lives all the way at the other end of the hollow through the woods. But I was about the head into the main village anyway, you're welcome to come along."

I was eager to rest my aching feet, so I eagerly hopped into his wagon that sat in front of his little cottage. "Is there only one road into Sleepy Hollow?" I asked, surveying the area from my higher perch and finding no other breaks in the fields around me.

"Indeed," Ezra said. He gave a 'tsch' to his mule, and the cart cavorted down the dirt road. I was thankful for the cushion of the straw beneath me to balance out the ruts and bumps. "One main road, and almost all of the houses are in the center of the town. Road goes right through the middle of it. If you keep following it through the forest, you'll get to the Van Tassel estate. Baltus is sometimes in town, or his daughter is, so you'll be able to talk to them without having to make the full journey."

"This is quite a lovely place," I commented. The houses were sturdy, though a bit old-fashioned looking. Not that that was unusual in the countryside.

"Very lovely," Ezra agreed. "A nice place to live, it is. Sleepy Hollow is one of those places you'll want to stay for your entire life."

I laughed at that. "I do like to travel, but I certainly do not mind putting down roots for a few seasons."

Ezra went quiet after that, and I contented myself with watching the farmland turn quickly into a more residential area. I could see a windmill off toward the Hudson, no doubt to catch the breeze from the river to move the sails. Small shops and homes began to show up, and people in the gardens or along the way stopped to raise their heads and stare at me. The progression of expression was almost always the same. At first, shock, and then, delight. I supposed strangers were not common to this area, especially as the Van Houtens had told me that no one had ventured up this way once the war ended, which would have been almost seven years now.

Upon reaching the main square of the town, Ezra pulled to a halt, and I jumped down from the wagon, giving him a bow. "My appreciation, good sir," I said. He nodded and doffed his cap at me, and then, with another flick of his reins, he and his cart went about their business.

The main street of the town was not large. I was sure that the population of it was not anywhere equal to that of Tarry Town. Perhaps my stay here would not be overly long. But the townsfolk were all eager to talk to me, to find out who I was, where I had come from, if I had family in the area, how long I planned on staying. Within only a few minutes, I had an offering for my night's lodgings. It was the custom of a traveling schoolmaster to be set up in the homes of one of his students for a week at a time before moving on to the next one. There were about a dozen elementary-age children in Sleepy Hollow, from what I could glean from the information being thrown at me, and that suited me just fine.

Two days later, I met with Baltus Van Tassel. He was the richest man in the village, and quite possibly in the entire area of the Hudson. He seemed to be the honorary mayor of Sleepy Hollow, though neither he nor anyone in the town called him by so formal a title. He was older than I expected, though he admitted to me that he had made his fortune before deciding to settle down and have a family. His cheery, blue eyes glimmered as we talked over dinner at one of the taverns. I came to learn that the whole glen of Sleepy

Hollow was quite self-sufficient. There were several freshwater springs that provided clean drinking water, and plenty of water from the Hudson as well. Several families raised sheep, cows, chickens, and pigs. There was a mill for grinding wheat, and homespun clothing was made from wool and cotton. There was a butcher for slaughtering the animals, whether livestock or hunted in the forest. Many kinds of crops grew in the area as well. Corn and wheat, as I had seen, but also pumpkins and watermelons, berries from the forest, apples in a small orchard, and all manner of vegetables. Each person in Sleepy Hollow had their tasks to perform, and it seemed that the entire town lived in a sort of peaceful harmony of sharing and camaraderie.

A few days after meeting Baltus, I met his daughter, Katrina Van Tassel. While I had never been much tempted by carnal desires, I had to admit that Katrina was stunning. With blond hair, bright blue eyes, a trim waist, and round hips, she was the sort of young woman any man would envy to have for a wife. I first saw her in the town at one of the shops, being followed by three or four young men who took turns fawning over her and assisting her with whatever she needed. When her eyes met mine, she stopped short, and I also did so myself, transfixed by that intense, blue gaze and the surprised smile that crossed her full lips. She crossed over to me while the gaggle of men behind her huddled and stared and whispered. I was still quite new to the town, so I was used to much whispering and furtive glances following me.

When she was in front of me, she smiled again, her cheeks dimpling in an endearing way. "You must be the new schoolmaster I have heard about," she said, her voice clear and tinkling like a crystal bell.

"Yes, madam," I said, giving her a small bow. "Ichabod Crane."

She giggled and held out her hand, which I took and pressed a kiss to the back of, as propriety dictated. "Katrina Van Tassel."

"A pleasure to meet you, Miss Van Tassel." Her skin was warm and smelled of honeysuckle and pine.

"And you, Master Crane," she said, giving a slight flutter of her lashes, her hand still gripping mine. "I do hope you will stay in Sleepy Hollow with us for a while, that we may be better acquainted."

"I intend to," I said, giving her a slightly shy smile. Despite her being quite a bit shorter than I, she still felt like a dominating presence. "I hope to stay at least until the fall, perhaps longer if my services are required."

"Oh, you must stay through the winter!" Katrina said with a breathy gasp. "I am certain your... services would be appreciated. It can be so dull in this quiet, little town."

I smiled, feeling myself utterly besotted like a lovestruck schoolgirl. "If I am welcome."

"Of course, you are welcome!" Katrina said and giggled softly again. "If you have need of anything at all, please do not hesitate to ask. We would be delighted to assist you."

"I thank you, Miss Van Tassel," I said, grinning like a fool. She lifted her hand that was still wrapped around mine, and I kissed the back of it with much more gusto. "It was a pleasure meeting you."

"The pleasure was mine," she said, giving me another dazzling smile before going back to her shopping, her gaggle of young men once more in tow.

I found myself almost always thinking of Katrina beyond that first encounter. I was under her spell, drawn like a bee to a flower. It seemed that whenever I was on the verge of being able to stop thinking about her, she would appear again, and the fantastic heavenly feeling would return. Only a few weeks after my arrival, she discovered that I was an accomplished piano player and singer, and she insisted that I come by the Van Tassel estate for weekly lessons.

The Van Tassel home was the largest in the area, surrounded by all manner of grain fields and dotted with smaller buildings full of animals. It was a lovely farm, made all the more beautiful by Katrina herself, the bucolic maiden, helping to tend the farm when she was not in the town. I worried that Baltus would perhaps see it as improper that I instruct his marriageable-age daughter, especially alone in the parlor as we often were, but he only chuckled and waved the concern aside with a knowing look and a stern finger-wagging at Katrina to behave herself, though none for me.

The other person whom I encountered frequently was a young man by the name of Abraham Von Brunt, otherwise affectionately known about the hollow as "Brom Bones." He was a gargoyle of a man, with broad shoulders, a square jaw, and a slightly mashed nose, though one could consider him handsome in a rugged sort of way. He was an accomplished horseman and hunter, and it seemed one of his daily missions was to watch me. There was jealousy in his dark eyes whenever he saw me talking to Katrina in town, and while he took pains not to draw my attention, I knew he often did impressions of my gawkiness or my city manners behind my back to his Sleepy Hollow Boys, as was called the group of young men who followed either him or Katrina around like a flock of geese, preening and flapping. Katrina sometimes berated him for these imitations, but it was in a teasing manner, and even I could see that her flirtations with him were of a more genuine nature than her interactions with the others in town.

So passed my late spring and summer in Sleepy Hollow. I stayed with various families, who were always willing to take me in. When I was not teaching, I did my best to make myself useful around the farmsteads, helping with the animals and vegetation where I could, though my knowledge of such things was fairly limited. But I instructed the children, and sometimes the wives, in the ways of literature and music, and my own repertoire of folklore and animal husbandry expanded in turn through their knowledge.

The months went by, and as the cooler weather of the autumn began to set in, the townsfolk began to chatter about the harvest party. I gleaned from the various gossip that it was the biggest event of the year in the village, hosted at the Van Tassel family farm on Halloween night, and everyone in the village was expected to attend. There would be food and dancing and much celebration for the bounty that blessed their small town to see them through the cold winter. Every time the harvest party was brought up in my presence, glances were cast at me, so much so that I began to feel like I was the centerpiece of the whole evening. I was unsure if I would be welcome at such a feast, as the newcomer to the town, but Katrina extended an invite to me personally one afternoon in early September, assuring me that my presence was absolutely wanted, and frankly, she required it. She held my hand as we spoke, and I was powerless to resist her request.

Chapter Two

I dressed in my best suit of black clothes the night of the Van Tassel harvest party, though that was not to say that my outfit was more ostentatious than any other, for a schoolmaster's wages were not much more than the food that he ate and the bed that he slept in. But still, I felt I must look my best with the whole town assembled in such a prestigious location as the Van Tassels'. Despite my protests that I was fine to walk the distance from one end of the hollow to the other through the winding forest path, I was provided an old plough horse named Gunpowder upon which to make my journey.

I might have made better time on foot than I did on the back of Gunpowder, for he was a brittle old thing, with one lame eye and a matted coat. But Hans Van Ripper, with whom I was currently staying, was insistent that, as the newest member of the town and unaccustomed to Van Tassel parties, I would welcome the company on the return trip. I took this to mean that the Van Tassels served excellent beer and cider, and while I did not plan to imbibe enough to make a fool of myself, my knowledge of alcoholic spirits was not extensive. I therefore set off to the Van Tassel farm on my once-noble steed.

The sun was just beginning to set when I reached the woods, through which I had to cross to reach the Van Tassel farm. I was not the most accomplished of horse riders myself, having grown up in the city, so as I crossed over one of the streams with its makeshift log bridge, I paused to let Gunpowder drink his fill of the cool water, as much a break for myself as for him. I did not dismount from his back, for while I was quite tall, he was taller still, and I was unsure if I would be able to get back on him without assistance.

As we stood at the edge of the stream, Gunpowder determined to drink his own weight in water, I felt a prickle at the back of my neck, just below my hairline. It was the feeling of being watched by an unseen entity, as if I were being studied. I twisted back and forth in my saddle, looking for the source of the uneasiness. I realized with a start that I had never been in the woods after sunset, and I had no idea what sort of creatures lurked in the foliage. I had never seen anything larger than a fox or squirrel, but the thought suddenly occurred that there might be something bigger amongst the brush and gnarled trunks. I had yet to see something as large as a bear or a wolf or a puma up close, and I had no weapon with which to defend myself, for the little good it might do me.

The feeling of eyes upon me intensified, and I scanned the shadowed limbs. I was so unsure what to look for, I might have passed right over a creature without seeing it, but still I found nothing of note. The tingling extended up my neck and into my scalp, my reddish hair nearly standing up on its own. I gave Gunpowder a kick to the ribs, which he ignored. I clicked my tongue at him, and one of his ragged ears flicked irritably, but he continued to drink.

My mind had started to recall the number of stories of spooks and spirits I had read so much about as a child and continued to enjoy in my later years. While I knew it was not likely that anything in these woods would be an unearthly beast bent on malicious intent, it still did not assuage the prickling of my skin that now spread down my arms under my black coat. A nearby rustle in the bushes drew my attention, my heartbeat intensifying in my chest. I half-expected to see a hungry wolf come bursting out of it.

Imagine my relief when what emerged from the bushes was a man and a woman with a small girl between them; it was the Von Brussetts with their little girl, Annabelle. They seemed a little surprised to see me in such a melancholy place on my melancholic ride. Annabelle gave me a hesitant smile, showing the gap where her two front milk teeth had fallen out. "Come along," Master Von Brussett said, giving her a pull and me a tight smile. "On your way to the Van Tassels', Master Crane?"

"Indeed," I replied, giving Gunpowder another kick. "Shall I accompany you?"

"Oh no, take your time," Von Brussett said as they passed me. "We'll all be there." And then they disappeared into the trees, leaving me once more alone in the woods.

The feeling of being watched had not gone with the departure of the Von Brussetts, and I shivered as a cool wind whipped through the air, snapping branches and spinning leaves. The cold months would be settling in with quite a kick, I was sure.

Gunpowder finally seemed to have drunk his fill, and he ambled up the bank and onto the forest path again. We reached a fork in the road, the left of which would take me to the Van Tassel farm. I had never taken the path to the right. When I had asked the townsfolk what lay in that direction, there had been uneasy glances, followed by Brom telling me, "The wooden bridge, and the old, abandoned church and graveyard."

I had not heard about a church in the vicinity. As I was not interested in continuing to pursue my father's zealotry, I had had no need to search for a congregation to join upon my arrival in Sleepy Hollow, and no one had seemed to begrudge me spending my Sundays in literature rather than the word of God. There was not a church in the village, and I assumed that if there was a Sunday gathering, it was in one of the homes, as was often the case in smaller towns. I also realized after having been told about the abandoned location that there was not a visible cemetery in the village either, which struck me as slightly odd. Regardless of how small the population of a few dozen people might be, there was sure to be death in some manner visited upon them and a need for some place to ensconce the departed. Perhaps there was a place in the forest designated as such, and, as an outsider, I was not privy to that information. There had been no deaths in the village in the time I had been there either, so it was possible the townsfolk had not given it much thought on my behalf.

Gunpowder stopped at the intersection of the road forks, leaning down to chew some clover he found there, and I felt a bead of sweat form at the back of my neck and roll down my spine. I could not see the bridge or the church from where we stood, and indeed, I did not feel the urge to do so either. My skin was already starting to crawl, as if invisible spiders were moving over my flesh. I gave Gunpowder a nudge that he ignored. The feeling of being watched intensified so much that I literally cracked my back swiveling around in the saddle to see if someone were right behind me. Of course, there was nothing, besides a gust of wind that blew some orange and brown leaves across the path. I gave Gunpowder a much sharper kick, and something in that intensity must have gotten through to him, because he began to trot on again and did not stop again until we reached the Van Tassel farmstead.

The lights burned within the stately manor home from dozens of candles and lamps. It cast a cheery glow over what was otherwise a chilly autumn night. Raucous laughter and singing came from within, and I dismounted and tied up Gunpowder with the relief of a man returning from war. I stepped inside the main room of the merry house to a spectacle of bounty as such that I had never seen, even in my hometown during the Christmas season.

Lamps, candles, and carved gourds were on every available surface and in every corner, casting cheerful flickers across the floor and walls, ascending up into darkness in the eves above our heads. A long table had been laid with the most sumptuous feast I had ever laid eyes on, the smell of smoked and roasted meats, buttered vegetables, steaming fish, and fresh pastries creating a mouth-watering ambrosia of scent. Barrels of ale and cider stood tapped around the room. A band played music in the corner, a fiddle and a drum and a fife, and couples caroused nearby in a wanton whirl of gingham fabrics and shined shoes. Several small children and dogs chased each other, weaving through the dancers like through a field of corn, the children shrieking with laughter, the dogs barking and wagging their tails as they waited for tasty morsels to be dropped by tipsy guests.

Baltus Van Tassel, in an embroidered waistcoat, stood by the fireplace, smoking a pipe and laughing with several other members of the town, and he lifted his hand in greeting when he saw me. And then Katrina appeared at my side, a vision of loveliness in a pink frock with a wide, white petticoat under it. "Master Crane," she cooed, latching onto my arm like a newlywed. "I am so pleased you were able to join us!"

I gave her a smile and lifted her hand to kiss it. "I thank you again for the invitation, Miss Van Tassel."

She giggled and batted her lashes. "Please, eat your fill, and then you shall dance with me. We must make merry."

I did not need to be told twice to eat, for while I was tall and lanky, I could hold the food of a man twice my size, and I could already see a platter of cheeses and deviled eggs that were calling to me. I wasted no time in packing my plate, only stopping when it felt like it would no longer be a polite amount for a single helping. I sat down on a nearby bench to eat and watched the dancers whirl around me.

Brom dropped onto the seat next to me, a tankard of ale in his hand. He slapped me jovially on the back, and I watched in dismay as a piece of smoked ham flew off my plate and onto the floor, where it was snapped up by one of the sheepherding border collies. "Glad you could make it, Crane," he said in his booming voice.

My shoulder stung from his friendly greeting, but I simply smiled. "Thank you. This is quite the gathering."

He grabbed one of my hands and pressed the mug into it. "Drink up."

I took it politely before he stood and sauntered away, going over to give Katrina a peck on the cheek. She playfully smacked his arm, and he gave me a knowing grin. I set aside the glass of ale and continued to eat the plate of food, all of which was quite magnificent. When my plate was clean, I returned for seconds, and, admittedly, thirds. I took one small glass of cider, but that was all the spirits that I consumed. It felt best to keep my wits about me, seeing as the entire village was here, and I was supposed to be a model of good character and sound reasoning for the children.

I watched Katrina throughout the evening. She looked a little more pallid than she had been throughout the summer, but I was sure preparing for such a lavish gathering was quite taxing. She was still a vision of loveliness, the perfect hostess, and she danced with nearly every man in the room, married or not. By the time I had worked my way through the myriad of pies and cakes and was feeling slightly sticky and in a bit of a stupor, she appeared in front of me, holding out her hands. "You owe me a dance, Master Crane."

I got to my feet, grateful now for only the single glass of cider in my full stomach as I led her to the dance floor. Heads turned to look at us, whistles breaking out from a few of the assembled watchers. The dances they had done were not unfamiliar, though a bit more old-fashioned than the more modern dances I was used to in the city, but I dutifully slid my hands into Katrina's and began to move with her across the floor. Despite my large feet and her petite stature, we cavorted together splendidly, the crowd clapping and cheering us on. I twirled her, her dress spinning and catching the firelight, and she was mesmerizing.

As she pressed in close to me again, her body warm against my own, I wondered if I perhaps felt something for her. She was certainly beautiful, even if she looked a little drawn in the firelight. There was no doubt that we got along just fine together. I had not given much thought yet to marriage or starting a family, only having been away from my father for a few short years, and while the idea of having my own little ones running around did not cause me apprehension, I could not picture what my wife would look like. Katrina would make a fine wife, if both she and I agreed to such a match, but I was not about to fool myself with silly daydreams. I was the outsider, and even if I decided to remain in Sleepy Hollow for a long time to come, I still would never fully be one of them. Not like the Van Tassels, or Brom, who was obviously sweet on Katrina. Nor did I wish to cause any upset between myself and the repugnant young buck. If Katrina felt anything for me beyond a kindredship for music and literature, she had not made it obvious to me.

The song wound to a conclusion, and Katrina curtsied to me in such a demure manner that I felt obliged to offer a flamboyant bow, lest anyone think my intentions to her were unbecoming. She giggled, and then another man had stepped forward and offered his elbow to her.

I found myself shunted to the side of the dancers, and then the meaty arm of Brom went around my shoulders, pulling me in for what seemed like friendly camaraderie, but a few inches more, and he would have choked the breath from me. "Sweetest country rose you ever did see, eh, Ichabod?" he chuckled, reeking of ale and woodsmoke.

I laughed uneasily. "Yes, I suppose she is."

His finger suddenly jabbed into my ribs with a ferocity that I felt was unwarranted, enough that it made me wince. "You suppose? Come now, man, art thou blind?"

I clicked my tongue, trying to pull away from Brom's ruthless grip. It felt like he was perhaps trying to trap me, to get me to say something about Katrina that would allow him to call me out to defend her honor. I was unsure how to redirect his concerns, so I ventured, "I doubt very much that she would have me over a strapping man such as yourself."

"Oh-ho, is that your game?" Brom asked. He took several steps back, and I was forced to follow with him or be dragged. We melted back into the shadows at the edge of the crowd. I tried to dislodge his arm from about my shoulders, but he held me fast. "Tell me, Ichabod Crane. What is it that draws your fancies at night, alone, in the dark?" His other hand suddenly pressed to my chest, his fingertips digging into my breastbone in a way that nearly folded me over like a paper version of my namesake. "Do you lust for Katrina? To feel those plump lips seal around your cock, those legs around your waist?"

His words made my face burn in humiliation and anger. I knew some men to be scoundrels, but I prided myself with being a man above such offensive mannerisms. "You would be wise to hold your tongue, sir," I said to Brom, stiffening in his grip.

He leaned so close that I could see the light sheen of sweat on his forehead. "Would I? Or have I read you wrong, *sir*, and you wish to feel a different sort of mouth around your cock?" His fingers skimmed down my chest and stomach. I felt like the floor had dropped from beneath me as I realized what he was implying.

"Remove your hands from me," I said.

Surprisingly, his hand stilled, though his fingertips still rested at the level of my navel. "Come now, Ichabod, surely you desire to have a peek between someone's legs. Katrina's? Mine? Would you care to watch? Or... perhaps join in?" His mouth was so close to my ear that I felt the brush of his lips against it, and I jerked back, throwing up my hands in an attempt to shove him away.

"I said, remove your hands, Abraham Von Brunt," I said, hissing through my teeth like a soaked cat, though both of us knew my threats were empty.

Brom chuckled. "Do not play coy with me, Crane. Surely you've explored the desires of the flesh, slaked your lust between a pair of wet thighs?"

The revulsion and horror on my face must have given him an answer, because he drew back with a bark of laughter. "God be damned, Ichabod Crane, you're a virgin!"

Several heads turned in our direction, and I felt for a moment that I might flee the house in embarrassment. Not shame, for I did not think that a man needed to throw himself at every pretty creature who beckoned, but neither did it seem like anyone else's business to know, and certainly not the entire gathered town. Brom laughed and slapped my shoulder again. "What do you say, man? Shall we show you what you're missing?"

I glared at him. "That is enough out of you, Brom Bones," I said, as if he were a misbehaving student. "I have no interest in your business, and I will thank you to keep your nose out of mine."

Brom chuckled, his dark eyes gleaming with mischief, but he took a step back, allowing me to at least take a full breath and straighten my shoulders. I was taller than him by several inches, but I knew he would still easily best me in a fight, and I had no desire to come to blows at a party where I was outside the inner circle. He gave me a small, mocking bow. "As you wish, my Lord Crane." Then he turned and vanished into the crowd.

I felt my jaw tighten, and the desire to leave the festivities and return to my quiet sanctuary at the Van Ripper home was growing more overwhelming by the minute. But the press of bodies gathered near the doorways precluded me to make any sort of graceful exit, and I was eventually drawn as an unwilling participant into a conversation with Baltus and several of the elder villagers. I stood by the fireplace, overheating in my jacket as I tried to listen politely. But I instead found myself staring at a decoration on the mantle that boasted large sunflowers, small gourds, and, in the midst of all of it, an ivory-colored human-like skull. I stared at it in curious fascination until I was asked to dance with several of my students, and my sour mood eventually mellowed as the little girls giggled and gave me hugs about the waist before running back to their mothers.

By and by, the dancing died down, and people set about to chatting. There were brief mentions of the war that had occurred not so very many years ago, but as the candles burned lower and dimmer, casting more menacing shadows upon the great room's walls, there came tales of the spirits and spooks and haunts of Sleepy Hollow. I had heard some of these tales before, for the people of Sleepy Hollow seemed to be quite the superstitious bunch. Something about this region, in its seclusion, carried an atmosphere of dreams and fancies that infected the town. But then came a new tale I had not heard before, one that shook me to the very marrow in my bones.

Brom leaped upon a chair in the center of the room, drawing all attention to him. Despite the copious amount of drink he had imbibed, he seemed strangely sober now, scanning the room with his dark eyes. "The Horseman comes," he said as the room quieted, and several soft gasps escaped from the crowd. I sat to the side, half in shadow, penned in by bodies on either side of me, securing me to my seat as Brom began his dark tale.

"Down the fork in the road, and across the covered wooden bridge lies the small, whitewashed church and cemetery. There is the haunt of the headless rider. A horseman, dressed in black, and driving forth a steed darker than the shadows of Hell. No one knows who he is or where he came from. Every year, on Halloween night, he rides through the Hollow. Every year, he strikes down a someone in the glen, consuming their soul and taking their head for his own." His dark eyes glittered with mischief as he scanned the crowd, lighting on me for the briefest moment, and I felt a drop of sweat form on the back of my neck.

"Who will be the sacrifice this year?" Brom continued. My eyes darted around the room. Every single person was transfixed, staring unblinking at Brom, as still as statues. "Who will the Horseman take as his conquest? Whose soul will he drag to hell in payment for the loss of his head?" The bead of sweat rolled under the collar of my shirt, making its way down my spine like an ice drop.

Brom's shadow flickered upon the wall in the dying light of the candles, and his large shoulders and hunched back looked positively monstrous over the wooden beams. "There must always be a sacrifice for the Horseman," he said, jumping lightly down from the chair and turning in a wide circle to encompass every person in the room with his gaze. "Without his yearly tithe of blood, he will ride through the Hollow and slaughter us all. When you hear his horse's hooves on the path, it is too late. The Horseman comes. For you!" He whirled around and yelled this last line at one of the little boys on the edge of the group. The boy screamed, and whatever spell had held the crowd entranced suddenly broke. The lights seemed to flare a little brighter, and the townsfolk began to laugh and chatter again.

I realized now that Brom's story had been nothing more than that, a ghost story to chill the blood of the partygoers, to frighten the children. And I had allowed myself to get caught up in it like a short-pantsed schoolboy. My discomfort with Brom had manifested his spooky tale into something other than the folkloric yarn it actually was. I found myself back at the dining table, trying to suppress the unrest in my body with all manner of sweet and delectable treats.

The crowd began to thin, with people starting to make their way home. Some rode in wagons, others upon horseback. While the arrivals for the party at the Van Tassel farm had been a trickle, the departure now felt like the floodgates had opened. Beyond the windows, the world outside was pitch black, made even blacker by the looming forest that blocked out the stars. My heartbeat picked up a little in my chest as I realized that I was going to have to take Gunpowder all the way through the forest, back to the Van Ripper farm, which lay at the complete opposite end of the hollow from the Van Tassel estate. I began to wish I had taken my leave much earlier, when Brom had accosted me, but there was nothing to be done for it now.

Katrina suddenly appeared at my side, catching my hand in hers. "Master Crane," she cooed. "What did you think of our little gathering?"

I gave her a polite smile. "It was the most lavish of festivities, Miss Van Tassel. You have my gratitude for inviting me to celebrate."

"Of course. You're a member of this town now, are you not?" she asked, her lashes fluttering a little.

I blushed a bit at that. "For now," I said.

"Then of course you are welcome," Katrina said. She moved closer, and suddenly her warm breasts were pressed to my arm through my jacket. "Brom has told me that you might be interested in a late-night rendezvous."

My stomach plummeted, and I forced a smile I did not feel. Katrina Van Tassel was my hostess and the daughter of the richest man in the hollow; I could not afford to treat her with disrespect. I also did not wish to make myself appear foolish, depending what Brom had told her. "I apologize, my lady. I do not know what Master Von Brunt has told you, but I believe there to have been a miscommunication between us."

Katrina batted her lashes again, pressing closer to me. "Is that so? Does that mean you do not wish to stay here with us tonight, Master Crane?"

My heart picked up in my chest. She was quite beautiful, and I am not ashamed to admit that I did consider her offer for a moment. But something about her, not just Brom's goading, felt wrong, though I could not say what it was. A shiver ran through my body, but I forced myself to not let it show. "Thank you, my lady, but no. I should return to the Van Ripper farm."

Katrina's full lips turned down in a pout, but I would not allow her to guilt me in this decision. "Are you sure?" Her hand slid up to press lightly against my chest, and my heart gave a sudden sharp beat under her palm that sent me back a step and made my breath catch in my throat.

"Yes, I am sure," I said, trying to give her a polite smile, my hand moving up to rub lightly at the spot where my heart had flared beneath her touch.

"As you wish," she said, releasing me. "Good night, Ichabod Crane."

"Good night." I drew back from her, aware that there were suddenly very few people about in the room. It appeared to be myself, Katrina, Baltus, and Brom. Brom was sitting in a chair by the fire, nursing another cup of ale. Baltus sat nearby, smoking his pipe and watching Katrina and I with a small, knowing smile. I gave them both a polite bow. "Good night."

They both nodded to me, and I excused myself from their presence. Stepping from the warm, candlelit house into the cool, dark night was like being plunged into the icy waters of the Hudson. I followed the lamplight to the stables where Gunpowder was snoring to wake the dead. I roused him, and he snorted in his grumpy way, but I did not care. I was eager to be as far away from the Van Tassel estate as I could get. My skin was still crawling, and I could not figure out why. Surely the prospect of spending the night in bed with Katrina and possibly Brom couldn't have disturbed me that much.

I saddled Gunpowder faster than I knew was possible, and then I gave him a kick in the ribs to get him to walk. He ignored my first one, and I was obliged to kick him harder, at which he set off at a speed similar to a summer mosey through the gardens. I would have been faster on foot. "Come on, now, boy," I prompted him, giving him a scratch on the ear and regretting I had not saved some of the feast's produce for him. "Let's get you home, and then I'll get you a lump of sugar. Two lumps if you pick up the pace." Gunpowder thought about this for a moment, then seemed satisfied with our deal, his steps hastening a little as he trotted past the fields that surrounded the Van Tassel farm.

I had not thought that I had left the estate that much later than anyone else, but the road was completely deserted, no signs of life anywhere besides the night crickets and the occasional swoop of a bird overhead. Even the woods leading back to the town seemed empty. No lights flickered from torches or lanterns, no voices shouted back and forth to one another or scolded noisy children. As Gunpowder and I approached the tree line, I felt my heart pick up in my chest, and I very nearly turned back. The thought that drove me forward was the smug satisfaction that would be on Brom's face, knowing he had scared me with his story of the headless rider. Facing him and Katrina after my rather vehement objections to their proposal was also not something I wanted to do.

The wind blew chilling fingers over me as the path around me grew suddenly darker, the trees forming a barrier overhead that only sent dappled bits of moonlight through them. I realized that I didn't know if horses had better night vision than humans, and even less so Gunpowder with his one murky eye. I gave him a nudge with my heel. "Come on, Gunpowder, old boy. Let's hurry through these woods and get home."

Gunpowder let out a rusty-sounding snort, as if to tell me he had already picked up his pace for me. I gave his neck a reassuring pat, more for my own comfort than his. There was only darkness behind me now, the Van Tassel manor lost to view through the trees, no more anchoring candlelight. Every movement of the wind caught my attention. Every shadow along the side of the road sent my eyes skittering about. Every story I had heard from the townspeople about spooks and haunts and spirits in these woods suddenly whirled about in my head like a tornado. And at the center of it was the specter of Brom's tale, the Headless Horseman, seeking out a blood sacrifice every year for the loss of his head. My heart gave another sharp beat in my chest, like it had when Katrina had laid her hand upon it, enough that it made me double over on Gunpowder's back, gasping for breath.

Something large overhead blotted out the moonlight, plunging me for a moment into deep darkness. I looked up, but the sky was suddenly clear again. I swallowed hard and urged Gunpowder on, my ears strained for any sound beyond the clomp of his hooves and the rustle of the wind. I wished now more than ever that I had thought to bring a lantern with me for the return trip, for while the swollen moon overhead was doing its best to light my way, even it seemed to have abandoned me to the darkness of the forest.

I rounded one of the large trees that bisected the path. Gunpowder stopped as short, and I stiffened atop him. A figure was at the side of the road, a few paces into the trees. Cloaked in shadow, I could not make out much beyond that it was someone on horseback. Gunpowder snorted and danced a few steps away from the figure, nearly off the path. I gripped the reins so as not to fall off at the movement, unable to tear my eyes from the form. I could feel eyes upon me, though the shadowed rider did not move as Gunpowder trotted warily past. Despite only being a few arms' lengths away, I still could not make out any features besides the legs and trunk of a large, dark horse, and someone astride it. My thought then was not of the supernatural, but that one of the partygoers had gone off the path for personal business and was now returning. I very nearly called out to see if perhaps there had been trouble when my heart gave another ferocious beat in my chest.

As if he had felt the single reverberation of my heart, Gunpowder suddenly picked up speed, so much so that I nearly tumbled off of him. Once I had righted myself sturdily, I looked over to see the horse and rider trotting along through the trees, keeping pace with us as the large horse navigated around the trunks with ease despite its bulk. My heart gave another painful thump, and this time a lump of fear rose in my throat. Why, I did not know, but my body knew something my brain did not, which was all the more frightening. "Who are you?" I demanded.

I received no answer. I asked again, bolder now, though I knew in my heart I would not get a reply. From what I could perceive, the figure did not even turn my way when I spoke, simply trotted along in the darkness near me, keeping pace with Gunpowder no matter what speed he took.

The gurgling of an approaching brook should have been reassuring, but even its slosh made the hair on my head stand up in fright. At this point I was certain that my strange midnight companion was not human. That thought chilled me to my very core, and I very nearly laughed out loud at the absurdity of the situation. Gunpowder and I crossed the brook that was no more than ankle deep, and I chanced a glance to the side again to see that the rider and horse had vanished. I had no more let out a sigh of relief when a plashy tramp sounded behind me, and I turned to see the figure only a few paces behind me, on the path now. His horse had just crested the bank when a patch of clouds slid away from the moon enough to illuminate my follower and his steed.

Despite what I had already known in my heart, seeing the headless rider atop the shadowy horse sent a jolt of fear down my spine as I had never experienced before. I think I must have screamed, for suddenly the woods were echoing with noise, and Gunpowder took off at a clip so fast that he nearly pitched me from the saddle. His hooves pounded down the path as if the very devil were at his heels, but I could hear thundering behind me and knew that the black steed and rider were matching me pace for pace. I heard the snort and chuff of the ink-dark animal and was almost sure I could feel its hot breath against my back as Gunpowder ran for his miserable life.

Something behind me screeched, like a giant bird of prey, the sound raising every hair on my body. It was as if the woods were alive with thundering hoofbeats, the wild screaming of Gunpowder, the snuffling and growling and frightful whinnying coming from behind me. I was bent so low over Gunpowder's neck that I couldn't even attempt to look over my shoulder, only the cacophony of sounds behind me telling me where my pursuer was.

We came upon the fork in the road, the right of which would take us back toward the village and potential safety. Imagine my shock and horror when Gunpowder turned to the left and plunged down the dirt path, kicking up rocks and mud in his wake. I think I must have shouted to him, but he was beyond hearing, panting and making the most frightful noises. I suddenly felt the saddle slip to one side down his bony ribs. I clutched at the pommel to try to save it, but it nearly dragged me off of him, and I was forced to let it go and wrap my arms around Gunpowder's neck so as not to be flung off. I heard the saddle hit the ground, and then heard it being kicked and trampled under the foot of the massive horse pursuing me. The strangest thought came to the forefront of my mind then, that Van Ripper would be upset over the loss of his saddle, and I would have to find a way to pay him back for it. Why that was what occupied me in that moment, I could not say. I clung to Gunpowder's neck like a babe to its mother, jouncing this way and that with prodigious violence, wondering if, with the right angle of my body against the sharp ridge of his backbone, he might cleave me asunder.

Something swiped through the air, so close to me that I felt it skim the side of my head and heard the swish of it deep in my ear. I could not see what it was, but the splintering sound that followed right behind it told me that whatever it was had struck a tree and gouged it. I imagined the Horseman wielding a mighty sword or ax, with which to take off my head with one blow, and I am certain that I screamed in terror, and an answering call went up behind me in response.

Up ahead I could see a covered wooden bridge, and beyond that, the gleam of faded, whitewashed walls that I assumed was the abandoned church. Despite having no reason to believe it so, I thought that crossing the bridge and into the hallowed churchyard might provide me safety from my terrible pursuer, whom I could still hear only a few gallops behind me. I clung to Gunpowder's neck with all of my strength as we hit the bridge, the sound of his running on the half-rotted boards deafening. It was not a superbly long bridge, and we burst out of the opposite end after only a few strides. It was when his feet hit the dirt path again that Gunpowder slowed to a stop, despite my desperate urging, wheezing and huffing, for he probably had not run so fast in his entire life. I turned to look behind me at the bridge, almost certain that the Horseman would be upon me in that very moment.

But, to my shock, the Horseman and his shadowy mount had stopped on the bridge, right in the middle. His body was turned away from me, as if looking at something behind him, and his horse stamped impatiently, as if it had been halted in the midst of a mad dash that it wished to continue. My heart suddenly slammed again into my ribcage with such force that I bent double, clutching at my chest with one hand, struggling to draw breath as terribly as the horse beneath me. The pain was so great that my vision blurred. My lungs felt as if they were clutched in the grip of a monstrous fist, my heart pounding like Gunpowder's racing hooves in my chest. The world suddenly tipped sideways, and I hit the dirt path. And then I knew only blackness.

Chapter Three

When I woke up, I was lying on something hard, but something had been draped over it. I forced my eyes open. The world was topsy-turvy. It was dark, and my eyes were unable to find something on which to focus to bring them into cooperation. I tried to reach up to rub them, only to find that my hands had been tied together at the wrists behind my back. The knot felt loose, the ropes barely clenching my skin. I then became aware of another sensation, that of something wet and cotton on my face. My tongue poked up to explore, and I realized with a startled gasp that there was a cloth tied around my mouth as a gag. It too was fairly loose, but panic still quickly set in as my body thought I was not drawing air into my lungs. I pushed myself from my side where I had been lying to full uprightness, giving a panicked yank at the rope around my wrist.

"Please, stay calm," came a voice from nearby that nearly made me leap out of my skin. I turned toward the sound, but my eyes could not penetrate the thick shadows that surrounded me. The voice was low and a little hoarse, with a bit of a Germanic accent to it.

I am not ashamed to admit that a whimper of fear escaped my throat as I thrashed at the rope.

"Please," came the voice again, in a tone that sounded like a farmer trying to soothe a frightened horse. "No harm will come to you."

My bound hands seemed to belie this statement, but though the cinch was not tight, I was not going to be able to get it off quickly by myself. My lungs fought for air again, and I closed my eyes to concentrate on taking a deep breath. The cotton gag in my mouth was damp with my own saliva, but my throat and nose were unobstructed. I inhaled, then let it out again. The next breath was easier, and now I could smell the air as my pounding heart began to slow. It was damp and a little musty, like inside of a root cellar, though without the fresh, earthy smell that accompanied vegetables. There was something in the air, almost sweet, but I could not determine what it was, though that was not my priority at the moment. I inhaled again, then exhaled, opening my eyes and turning them toward the darkness where the voice had come from. There was someone there. I could feel their presence, though I could see nothing more than a few steps beyond me. I glanced down to see that I was lying on what seemed to be a pile of blankets made into a make-shift bed. My legs were curled under me, as I had been lying in the fetal position upon waking, and I cautiously stretched them out, keeping them on the blankets as though they were a log raft upon a fierce river that would otherwise sweep me away. I turned my eyes to the darkness again, trying to soften my features from the panic that I was sure was still evident in my eyes and my tensed shoulders.

"I am sorry I had to tie you," said the voice, and it sounded genuinely remorseful. I could discern now that it was a male voice, world-weary and rough, but kind. I couldn't stop from making a muffled questioning sound through my nose. "I have much to explain. I know you saw me on the path, and I know my appearance can be shocking. But I swear that no harm will befall you, and your questions shall be answered. I can see you in this darkness, so nod if you understand me."

The blackness was so complete that I was unsure how any man could see more than a few steps from him. My breathing was still much too fast as I realized that the origin of the voice was none other than the haunted creature I had seen behind me as we crossed the stream. The singular glance I had seen under the moonlight had been enough to shake me to my very marrow. The only other vision I had was of the figure in the middle of the bridge, turned away from me, so much in silhouette that the form would not have been immediately clear to me had I not known.

I did not wish to see. Every fiber of my being resisted the desire to see my captor full revealed, as I sat here, bound, unable to scream or run, with very little of my own autonomy left. But sitting here in tense silence, knowing he was there, beyond my vision, was worse, so I hesitantly bobbed my chin once.

A window across the way from me was suddenly opened, flooding the space with blue moonlight. I flinched my head away, my eyes stinging for a moment at the unexpected brightness. I heard a lantern being lit. I was able to crack my eyes open again with less pain now. The lantern was suddenly lifted from what I assumed was a table, and I could see the vaguest outline of a figure. The lantern swung to face me, and I forced myself to focus beyond it so as not to hurt my eyes by staring into the glow. It drew closer, the rustle of footsteps over the ground as quiet as a church whisper. Out of the darkness slowly materialized an arm holding the lantern out, covered in what appeared to be a black coat with some sort of brass buttons on the sleeve. A step further, and the light began to illuminate a chest and lower torso, then traveled down to gleam off of polished riding boots. It was a broad chest, to be sure, strong and formidable. Another step closer, and the light slid further up the chest to the high-necked collar of the jacket. My eyes lifted to where the next step would reveal a face, but as the figure took another halting step toward me, the spot stayed in shadow. One step more, and my captor was revealed in full, only slightly more than an arm's length from me.

The collar of his black coat stood unsupported, for at the base of his throat, where his shoulders joined to create what should have been his neck, was nothing. It was such a sudden and unexpected blankness that I almost missed what was cradled in his left arm, held to his breast. It was a head, with deceptively bright eyes that were focused on me, the thin lips slightly parted to reveal the faint glint of teeth, dark hair, and sharp cheeks.

My breath caught, and I could not tell if my heart sped up or stopped altogether. I only know that in that moment, I was seeing the impossible, and I had to be dreaming. I thought I might have screamed through the gag around my mouth, but I slumped backward against the wall as the world went black again.

I do not know how long my mind kept itself in the fearful darkness, but when I became aware of my surroundings again, something soft and damp was pressing against my face, blotting away the heat from it. I was lying down on my side again, for my hands were still uselessly tied behind me. My eyes fluttered, and I first saw a heavy, black coat and trousers in front of me. A hand stroked the cooling cloth over my face again, and my gaze traveled up the sleeve to the shoulder, and then to nothingness again. I inhaled sharply, sure that I was not dreaming this time.

"Let me explain," came the accented voice. I turned to see that the lantern had been set nearby, moonlight still illuminating the small, wooden space with a high ceiling above me. Resting on the floor only a few paces from my own face, was a head. A head with dark hair tied back, though strands escaped and floated around the pale face. As I have mentioned, the eyes shone, as alive as any I had seen, the irises a very dark brown. The lips were thin, made thinner still by the fact that the lips were pursed in concern. The sunken look that accompanied death was not present in this head; if it were not for its utter lack of a body, I would not have given it a second thought.

And then the lips moved, the head shifting ever so slightly where it sat. "Let me explain," came that hoarse voice again, and I watched the words come from the head's lips that moved with perfect synchronicity. I stared in shock, then jumped as the cool cloth brushed over my hot neck, reminding me of the figure that knelt next to me in a state of decapitation that should not have been possible. It was indeed the Headless Horseman I had seen earlier in the woods, that pursued me through the trees and over the bridge toward the solitary, abandoned church. A whine involuntarily escaped my lips, over the gag that still prevented me from screaming, and I drew back from the hand with the damp cloth, though it admittedly did feel nice against my overheated skin.

The headless body moved back from me, giving me much-needed space. Then, while I watched in fascinated horror, it lifted its head up from the floor with both hands and held it in front of its chest like some sort of ancient sculpture of a Greek monster. My lungs felt tight, swelling into my throat until I thought I might choke, and I forced myself to breathe so as not to be lost once more to the blackness.

The dark eyes watched me for a moment before it spoke again. "I know my appearance is frightening, and for that, I offer my profound apologies." The words were so formal, in their slight accent, that it almost made me laugh despite the panic reeling through my body. But I knew if I started to laugh, I would not be able to stop, and I did not need madness to carry me away in this moment. "I promise you again that no harm shall befall you at my hands," the head said again, its eyes solemn as a prayer.

I swallowed and pushed myself up to a seated position on the ground, though my back remained pressed to the wood behind me. This put me nearly eye-level with the head held at the chest, for the Horseman was still on his knees from tending to me. The head cocked just a bit on its stump of a neck held in its own hands, which almost made me laugh again at the absurdity of the motion.

"I wish you to be comfortable. I will remove the gag if you swear you will not scream."

I blinked at the statement. Screaming was still an option, trapped in my throat as it was, but the ability to swallow and not feel so vulnerable outweighed it, and I slowly nodded my head. "I will undo it," the Horseman said, setting the head aside on the ground once more before the hands reached toward my face. I gave a startled gasp, and the hands drew back. "Shall I untie your hands, and you can remove it yourself?"

Somehow, the idea of turning my back on this figure once again was not more reassuring, so I just shook my head and tipped it a bit for better access to the knot behind me. The pale hands moved past me, the chest close to my face. I inhaled, expecting the smell of rot and decay, but there was nothing more than a faint, earthy smell, like newly-turned dirt in a cornfield. The knot loosened, and the gag fell away from my mouth. The urge to scream was renewed, but I forced myself to close my lips around it, swallowing it back with a mouthful of saliva. I licked my lips, and the Horseman pulled back.

"I will get you some water," the head offered, and I watched in fascinated horror as the body rose from the floor and walked back to the table by the window to pour a cup of water from a pitcher, leaving his head sitting next to the lantern, where it studied me curiously, as I studied it.

I had a thousand questions, unsure which was the most important, so I choked out the first one that I was able to form into a coherent sentence. "Your body can see without your head?"

The Horseman's head laughed. Genuinely laughed, the sound surprisingly pleasant despite its rasp, the eyes closing in mirth for a moment. "In a manner," he said. "It is more of a sense of things around me than actual vision, but I have lived here for a very long time."

"Where is 'here?'" I asked, licking my lips again.

"The old church," the Horseman said.

"Am I dead?"

"No," the Horseman reassured quickly, in a tone that was much gentler than I would have expected. "No, you are not." Movement caught my eye, and the headless body returned, a goblet in its hand. "I will untie you if you promise not to run," the head said.

Despite every fiber of my being telling me to throw myself to my feet and dash as if the very devil were after me, I merely nodded and shifted uneasily to present my hands to the figure. Fingers carefully undid the rope that held my wrists together, and the relief in my shoulders as it fell away was immediate. The body drew back, inclining its chest a bit at the goblet at my feet as it scooped up its head once more and sat down on the floor a few arms' lengths away.

I picked up the goblet with caution. My gaze did not leave the figure as I lifted it to my lips and swallowed the fresh, cool water inside. I drank the entire cup in a few swallows before putting it down by my feet again. And then, we stared at one another, silent as predator watching prey to see who would move first.

The silence stretched on for so long, no sound at all breaking it, that I almost wondered if I had gone deaf, before I finally forced out, "Are you going to kill me now?"

The Horseman stared at me in surprise, as if the question baffled him. "No."

"Then, why am I here?" I asked, feeling irritation start to rise in my chest.

"I saved you," the Horseman replied.

"From what?" I asked, feeling like I kept aiming for a bullseye and somehow missing the entire target.

"From her."

"Her who?"

"The witch."

These short responses were not helpful to either of us. I let out a long, frustrated sigh through my nose. "What are you talking about?"

The Horseman frowned, then lowered his eyes to stare at the wooden floor under us. "You are not dead. But you are also not entirely alive."

My chest tightened in further irritation. "Will you please speak plainly? I have no patience for mind games right now." My words came out sharper than I meant them to, surprising myself. I very rarely was so ungracious. Even moreso, it seemed foolish to rattle my mouth to a supernatural being whom I had every reason to assume was going to cut my head off.

"I am sorry. It has been so long since I have spoken with anyone." The crestfallen look on his face and the slump of his shoulders seemed to show genuine apology. "Let me start again. A powerful curse has been placed upon you."

I raised a brow at that. "A curse?" The Horseman's chin bobbed solemnly. "Who would place a curse on me?" I was nothing but a simple schoolmaster.

"Katrina Van Tassel," the Horseman said.

My breath left me in a snort of laughter. "What?"

"The Van Tassel family, Baltus and his daughter, are witches."

The words flew about my head like a company of bats as I tried to understand them. I could hardly say that witches were not real when I had undeniable proof of the supernatural sitting in front of me. "Witches?" I said, half question, half scoff. "Baltus Van Tassel is a wealthy landowner."

The Horseman stared at me, and I realized after an uncomfortable silence that being a rich elder in a town did not preclude one from dark magic. I sighed and rubbed at my eyes with my fingers.

"I am sorry, you are probably still much unnerved after this evening," the Horseman suddenly said. "I have much to share with you, but perhaps it would be better for you to rest."

"I'm fine." The words came out sharper than almost anything I had ever said in my life, and I froze at my own brevity. The Horseman did too. I felt a moment of selfish glee at having momentarily startled this supernatural being, but I had too many questions fighting for space in my mind to dwell upon it. "What does this curse do?"

"It powers the spell that shields Sleepy Hollow from the rest of the world," the Horseman said, his voice low, as if trying to not set me off again. "It protects this town. No one dies of old age or illness. The harvest is bountiful, the animals reproduce well. It is a haven from the rest of the world, trapped in time."

Had the man relating this information to me not been impossibly headless in front of me, I might have thought the whole thing no more than another folktale. But, even still, the idea that Sleepy Hollow was under the curse of a witch family to make it prosperous seemed downright absurd.

"Surely the townspeople know that this is an enchanted place?" I scoffed. "If they do not grow old or die?"

"The magic distorts their memories," the Horseman replied. "It has been this way for many years without change. Sleepy Hollow is trapped in time, as are all in it."

I heaved a rusty sigh. "Let me say, for the sake of this discussion, that I believe what you're saying is true. What happens to those she curses?"

The Horseman's voice became quieter. "After they leave the harvest party on Halloween night, she chases them through the forest. It is a game for her, hunting her victim like prey."

I recalled the screeching and rustling in the woods that had followed me. I had thought it to be the Horseman, but I wondered now if instead it had been Katrina, chasing after me as her dark magic festered inside of me. Of course, that was predicated on my believing what the Horseman was telling me. "And what happens if she catches them?" I asked.

The Horseman's body slumped a bit. "She decapitates them and uses their soul to power her magic for another year. The body is left for the villagers to find, but she takes their head away as her prize."

"But, she did not catch me," I said pointedly.

"The dark curse is still inside of you. It will drain your soul, piece by piece, as she needs it, instead of releasing to her all at once as it does when she kills her victim."

I remembered the cannon boom of my heart that had precluded me falling off of Gunpowder after I crossed the bridge, the head-splitting agony that had stolen my breath and sent me spiraling into darkness. Was that the magic inside of me, siphoning my soul like syrup from a tree? How often would I experience such torture? "What... what will happen to me?" I asked, licking my lips with my suddenly very dry tongue.

The Horseman was silent for a long moment, so long that I wondered if perhaps he did not know or did not care to answer, before he slowly said, "At midnight on Halloween night next year, whatever is left of your soul will leave your body, and you will die."

The world swam in front of my eyes, and I wavered in place for a moment, glad I was leaning against the wall or I might have toppled over. I had a year to live, in whatever half-life state this was as my soul was wrung from my body like water from a cloth.

The Horseman frowned, leaning in for a moment as if he wanted to put his hand on my shoulder, but I drew back with a sharp breath, and he returned to his spot again. "I am sorry. I know this is so much to understand after a very trying ordeal. Do you want to rest now?"

I did not know what I wanted. Suddenly being told that in a year I would die was hardly a place to end this conversation with this specter, but I did not know what else to say. Without thinking, my hand moved up to feel my own heart beating under my ribs. It felt no different than it ever did. Could there really be a dark curse inside of me, sapping my life from me? After a moment of me not answering him, the Horseman got to his feet and walked away. I watched him cross a short distance before he walked down a set of stairs and disappeared from view. I wanted to look to see where he had gone, but my whole form felt numb, and I simply sat and stared.

Chapter Four

I think I stayed in that spot for several days, for the light changed in the windows many times. The Horseman left me cups of water, plates of berries and clumsily-roasted meat, and a chamber pot. I felt exhausted and angry, and my body did not want to listen to my commands. I ached from my dash through the woods on Gunpowder. I vaguely wondered where the foolish creature had wandered off to, but that was hardly my priority now. I slept more than I ever had in my life, my whole body listless with something I could not name. It was not entirely fear, nor anger, nor despair, but a strange mixture of all and nothing. The Horseman did not speak to me, and I did not speak to him.

I eventually seemed to rouse from whatever stupor had fallen into. As I stood, I realized now that the low wall I had been leaning against was actually the loft at the back of what appeared to be the sanctuary of a small church. I turned to stare out over the space below me. Light streamed in through the windows where the wooden shutters had been opened. Across from me was a formal pulpit and sounding board, with a raised dais and kneeling rail. Looking straight down, I could see that the area that most likely had once been filled with wooden pews for worshippers only contained a few now, the rest seeming to have been cleared away.

I could see the Horseman, stretched out on one of these benches. His head was resting on his upper chest, and he held a book in front of him, appearing to be reading. The sight of it was so profoundly absurd that I nearly laughed. Instead, I crossed the gallery, realizing that there was also a lovely pipe organ up here as I went, to find the stairs that led downward. I took them carefully, each one creaking softly under my step. When I reached the bottom, I entered the sanctuary again. The Horseman had set down his book, and I could see him watching me, but he said nothing.

My eyes raked over the rows of pews, some of which had been removed to make a wider living space that was strewn with a few books, paper and quill, and other implements that spoke to someone living here. Scattered about were carved figurines of all sizes, from the size of my pinky to a nearly full-sized dog, in various levels of skill. When I reached the railing at the front of the sanctuary, I turned to gaze back at the congregation area and up to the balcony where the Horseman had made his comfortable nook next to the pipe organ. Some part of me wondered if it would still play after all of these years, or if the Horseman himself could play it. "Is this where you live?" I finally asked to break the silence that had stretched as I explored.

"Yes," he said, still half-reclined on the pew as he watched me.

I let my eyes roam for another moment before I heard him ask, "Are you hungry?"

I nodded slowly. The Horseman motioned to a door at the back of the sanctuary near the stairs. "Go refresh yourself, I will get you some food." He did not move from his spot on the pew until after I had stepped inside the small privy and closed the door. A lantern glowed warmly, and the room was at least warm and clean.

Once my business was completed and I had washed myself quickly with the pan of water there, I stepped out again and made my way back into the sanctuary area. The Horseman had set out a piece of cloth spread with some forest berries for me. "It is not much for now. I will get more for you when the sun goes down."

I ate quickly and swallowed the cup of water he left for me, and then we stared at one another again. "You have lived here alone, all of these years?" I asked when the silence became almost deafening.

He rose to his feet, holding his head in his hands at chest-level, and slowly approached me, as though he were the one invading my home instead of the other way around. "Nearly," he said.

I got to my feet as well, realizing that he was shorter than I, now that we were side by side, which was not unusual considering my beanpole frame. Even if his head had been attached to his shoulders, I figured he would still have been below my own height by an inch or two, which was a strange way to contemplate someone. He was much broader than I, with wide shoulders, a trim waist, and strong legs. He was dressed head to toe in black, from his collar to his boots. In the brighter light from the open windows, I could also see now that the place on his shoulders where his neck would have connected him was covered in a piece of black cloth, tucked in all the way around his upstanding collar. I wondered if that had been something he had done for himself, but that seemed like a rather rude and presumptuous question to ask.

"What do you mean, nearly?" I asked, turning my eyes upward to the gold candelabra that hung overhead.

"A few of the cursed individuals stayed with me, in the beginning," he said, and I detected something in his voice that sounded very much like discomfort.

"So I am not the first person you have saved from the witch on Halloween night."

"No," the Horseman said, his voice as morose as a eulogy.

"May I ask what happened?" I ventured, not entirely sure I wanted to hear, but I needed to know what fate would befall me now that my life had been spared for a year.

"The first year, the... forgive me, I cannot even remember now if it was man, woman, or child. But the sacrifice left the sacred grounds of the churchyard, and the witch slaughtered them by sundown. That was how I learned she could not pass the bridge; she waited, hidden, just beyond it until the sacrifice ran toward the village before she struck." The Horseman straightened a little, his mahogany eyes meeting mine. "The next year, I also saved the sacrifice. And the next year, and the next. But it never did any good. If I kept them here, they would die at midnight the following Halloween after long bouts of suffering, no matter how I wished to hold on to them. One year, the sacrifice was an orphaned girl of no more than ten who washed up after a boating accident. She stayed through the winter with me and then returned to the village in the spring. When the villagers saw her, they tied her to a stake and burned her alive in the square. I could hear her screams all the way here."

I inhaled sharply, reaching behind me to grasp the prayer railing of the dais, my stomach churning.

The Horseman's fingers twisted uneasily in a few of the strands of his long, dark hair. "I stopped trying to save them," he said softly. "I thought a quick death at the hands of the witch was more merciful than letting them suffer. And, as selfish as it is, I could not bear to watch any more of them die."

"What made you decide to save me then, instead of letting the witch have me?"

The Horseman was silent for a long time until his eyes broke apart from mine to look uneasily at the ground. "I do not know," he said. "I was drawn to you. I... wanted you. Wanted to protect you. Despite knowing what fate awaits you."

The words made no sense, and my eyes narrowed. "You wanted to protect me? From a curse that you tell me is draining my soul from my body every moment that I stand here?"

"Ichabod, please," the Horseman said, reaching out a pleading hand to me. "I know it is all hard to believe, but I-"

"How do you know my name?" I cut in with surprise. Names held power, and I was sure I had never once uttered my name in the presence of this ghoul.

The Horseman blinked. "What?"

"I have never given you my name," I said firmly. "So how do you know it?"

"I... I have known it from the day you arrived. Outsiders are not common in Sleepy Hollow. I heard whispers on the wind that a new schoolmaster arrived."

The words reminded me of the warning from the Tarry Town folk, that people who ventured into the northern area were not heard from again. "Was Halloween the first time you saw me?"

"No," the Horseman admitted after a pause. "I saw you many times, in the village. When I would ride through the forest, I would sometimes see you helping the farmers, or through the windows."

Realization rushed through me, followed by anger, hot and fetid, like venom spreading through my veins. "You watched me all of these months, and you never thought to warn me?"

"Warn you?" The Horseman sounded genuinely perplexed by the idea.

"To tell me that Katrina was planning to curse me? To let me know my life was in danger?"

The Horseman gestured with one hand to his form. "Do you think I could have approached you like this, and you would have listened to anything I had to say?"

I knew that his words were truth, but fury was beating behind my eyes, making my thoughts turn black and my heart churn with rage. "You could have done something! Warned the villagers, or sent me a note."

"The villagers would not help you," the Horseman said, his voice rising suddenly. "They are all under her spell, every last one of them."

I scoffed angrily at that. "Then I could have left on my own before the harvest party."

"Do you not think I didn't want to?" the Horseman asked, his eyes darkening slightly, his voice lowering. "If it would have done any good, I would have. But once you cross the line of magic into this glen, you become part of Sleepy Hollow, and you cannot leave. If you were to try, the magic would prevent you."

"What are you talking about?" I snapped.

"The same magic that keeps Sleepy Hollow suspended in time protects it from the outside world. If anyone crosses into its border, they are trapped here. She would have chosen you, regardless of what I might have said or done. Any outsiders to Sleepy Hollow are chosen as the sacrifice, that is the way it has always been."

"So you knew from the day I arrived that I was going to be the sacrifice to you, and you were lonely, so you decided that you would just let her curse me? To torture me and siphon my very soul from my body, so you would have someone to talk to for a year?" I was yelling now, my voice echoing off the beams of the church.

"I wanted to protect you!" The Horseman's voice rose in desperation to match mine. "I tried to save you!"

"Yet you knew I couldn't be saved once she cursed me," I hissed. "Do not pretend that your intention was pure."

The Horseman stared at me for a long moment before his shoulders slumped, suddenly seeming like his own weight was dragging him down. "I'm sorry," he said. "You are right. I chose my own selfishness over your suffering."

Something inside me twinged with regret. I could only imagine the depths of his loneliness here, night after night, year after year, with no one for company. I understood being alone with no one to talk to, though I could not know the magnitude of it. But just as quickly as it had come, the pang was gone, replaced by dagger-sharp fury once more.

The words left me before I could think about them. "You should have left me to die!" I snarled, whirling away from him and striding across the sanctuary toward the arched door of the church. He followed after me, matching my pace.

"Ichabod, wait. I know you are angry, but your soul is tethered to her, and she will use your emotions to try to draw you out of hiding. She will kill you."

"She will not!" I declared, swinging around to point one finger violently at him, instinctively pointing to where his face should have been and having to adjust it lower to the level of his chest where he held his head. "I will not let her. I will escape this place. I will leave Sleepy Hollow!"

"You will not." His voice was desperate now. "Please. Do not do this."

With a snarl, I turned and yanked open the heavy, wooden door. Sunlight flooded in, blinding after the muted light of the church, and I threw up an arm. It was then that I realized the entire churchyard, with its stone monuments to the dead, was covered in a layer of shining white, as was the bridge. The stream still flowed, but chunks of ice floated down it. My breath left my lungs in a puff.

The Horseman was next to me now. "Ichabod," he said, his voice firm. "Once you cross that bridge, she can reach you. She can kill you." He reached out his hand to grasp my arm, but I shoved it away, with enough force that he took a step back.

"She's going to kill me anyway," I said fiercely. "If I run now, I should make it to Tarry Town."

"You will not," the Horseman said, his voice cold and desperate. "I do not say this to trap you here. I say this to keep you alive."

"For how long? Until she saps all of my soul from me and leaves me a withered husk?" I demanded. I took a step outside, the snow crunching under my shoe, which was not meant for this sort of weather.

"Ichabod." His voice was pleading. "At least if you are going to run, wait until spring. You will freeze out there."

"I will go to the village," I replied firmly.

"No!" His declaration was so vehement that it stopped me in my tracks. "The villagers will be no friends to you. You are cursed, and they know it. They will burn you alive to pay the blood sacrifice."

A jolt of fear shot through me at that, but I could not let my determination be swayed. "At least I shall be warm then!" I snapped before turning on my heel. He might have responded, but I did not hear him over the stomp of my feet over the snow as I stormed down the church steps and through the pathway, the gravestones watching me depart in the silent gloom. I stepped through the picket fence that surrounded the churchyard and took a deep breath, inhaling the fresh, frosty air. It was icy cold, and I could feel the inside of my nose freeze with each breath I drew in. There was no sign of Gunpowder anywhere, not that I had expected him to simply be waiting where I had fallen however many nights ago. I strode toward the bridge, wanting to wrap my arms around myself, but I would not show the Horseman any weakness. I reached the bridge, peering through it to the bright opening at the other end. A part of me wanted to glance back, to see him watching me from the doorway, but I would not give him that satisfaction. I was going to leave Sleepy Hollow and its ridiculous tales of curses behind. I took one step onto the bare planks, then another. My feet left wet, snowy tracks for the first few paces as I started across the bridge. It was not very long, but it still felt as if I were walking for an eternity before I emerged out the other side into the sunlight once again.

I felt nothing different. No shift in the air, no change in my body. No creature or monster sprang from the brush to grab me, nothing stirred in the trees other than the wind. Lifting my head high, I started to walk. The church was to the east, the Van Tassel farm to the north, the Hudson River to the west, and the village to the south. After leaving the glen, I could head further south to Tarry Town, where I would be free from all of these spooks and spirits and nonsense. Away from Sleepy Hollow and the ridiculous folklore about blood curses and witch families. I started through the trees, unsure of the path, as the entire area was covered with snow, so I simply looked for where the area was clear and walked that way.

Once I was out of sight of the bridge, I wrapped my arms around myself. My black suit was not made for weather this ferocious, and I was already regretting my decision to leave without a blanket or coat of some kind. I realized I also had no food or water with me.

Water would be easy enough to procure, for the snow was pure in many places, but my stomach rumbled in such a way that it made me wonder if other creatures would think me a vicious beast in the forest.

My body grew heavier every step further I took from the church. Cold was settling in, and I feared that I might never get warm. I would have given the entirety of my meager belongings for a cup of hot chocolate and a warm bowl of rabbit stew. That brought back memories of the delicious food from the Van Tassel harvest party that I had gorged myself on. A last meal for a sacrificial lamb, if the Horseman's words had been true.

Something snapped in the trees nearby, and I whirled around, looking for any sign of movement, but there was none. I could see a little better with the sun than I could on that dark night I had set off to the Van Tassel party, but the woods were still full of shadows and unseen ghouls. I turned and picked up my pace, as fast as I dared without slipping on icy patches of ground.

I knew I had to be getting closer to the village. I could smell chimney smoke and some kind of roasting meat that made my mouth water. I heard the jingle of bells on a horse harness and the squeal of children as they played in the snow that I was so eager to escape from. I started toward the village. I would ask for a coat and something warm to eat, with the promise to return it, along with interest and my gratitude, once I reached Tarry Town.

A sudden shriek made me stop dead in my tracks, heart freezing solid in my chest. It was the sound of a little girl, and I pictured a burning pyre in the town square. And then I heard her wail

"Maaaaa!" in a plaintive tone that told me it was probably nothing more than a brother putting snow down the neck of his sister for fun. I unclenched my jaw and forced the air from my lungs as a large, warm burst. I was much jumpier than I thought I should have been. My nerves were so tight I might have played a concerto on them. I wondered if, in my hesitant state, it might be better to skirt the village rather than entering outright. I did not need the folk to see me as nervous as a rabbit or coiled as a snake. I would find a blanket in a barn and then return it later with a profound apology for my rudeness.

I slipped through the trees along the edge of the village. It was much quieter than it had been during the earlier months. I supposed the snow and cold had driven most people inside, since the land could not be planted or harvested during such a time. I found my way to one of the outer buildings toward the edge of the town. It was a storehouse with smoked meats and dried fruits and vegetables. I greedily ate my fill, making a mental note of every bite I took, that I might send payment to the Jansen family, whose building I currently squatted in. I found a small burlap sack and was filling it with cheese and meat when I heard footsteps approaching, and my heart thundered in my chest.

This was the moment, and I had to make a decision. I could step forth and reveal myself, or I could hide. I knew not which would be the wiser choice, but I had mere seconds to make it. It was possible the Horseman had made up the story to keep me with him, to keep me from asking for help to escape this place. Logic dictated that I could reveal myself later if I liked, but once I was found, there was no hiding again, so I dove behind several bags of potatoes and curled up, trying to make myself as small as possible with my gangly form. I heard not one, but two, voices outside the storehouse door before it creaked open, light spilling across the floor only a foot away from where I crouched.

"...in for a hard winter," said a voice that I recognized as Master Jansen.

There was a rustling, and I saw the shadows of the two men as they searched the shelves for something. I held my breath, sure my heartbeat might give me away.

A laugh resounded, that of Ezra Brouwer. "Maybe the snow came on so sudden because that boy's blood hasn't been spilled yet."

"They never did find that Ichabod Crane, did they?" Jansen asked.

"Nope. Just Hans's saddle, and that ragged old thing he calls a horse, wandering around the fork."

"You think he was able to cross the bridge to that old church?"

"Couldn't say, but s'pose it's possible," Ezra said.

"Would be odd for the Horseman to spirit him away entirely. Usually he only takes the head," Jansen said, a strained chuckle in his throat.

"You think maybe he escaped the hollow?"

"Naw. He's somewhere in the woods. The Horseman will have his head, like he always does."

"Wish he'd hurry up about it," Ezra sighed. "My ol' bones don't like this cold snap none."

"Feel free to go into the woods and look for him," Jansen said. "Maybe the Horseman's lost his touch this year."

"Buh," Ezra exhaled. "I hope that spook never comes after me."

"He wouldn't want your head, old man, you don't have a scrap of brains in it," Jansen said.

Ezra let out a guffaw of laughter. "You watch yourself, young pup. I ain't book smart, but I can still lick ya seven times til Sunday."

The door closed behind them again, plunging me into the semi-darkness of the storehouse's chinked logs. I heard their steps crunch away, but I dared not move, frozen to my spot in the darkness. The townspeople were against me too, knowing my blood had to be spilled as the sacrifice. I could not trust anyone in Sleepy Hollow, as the Horseman had said. I had to get away, as swiftly as I could.

I stayed still until everything had been quiet outside for a number of minutes, before I scooped up the small bag of provisions and grabbed a blanket that had been draped over a crate of apples. I checked through the cracks, finding no one nearby. I eased the door open, grateful in the moment for my slender build, before sliding out and closing the door again. I darted for the cover of the tree line, the blanket pulled over my head to hide my identity if anyone were to look outside. Once inside the trees, I turned south and began to run. I could stay off the road, in the trees, until I was sufficiently far enough away from Sleepy Hollow that no one would be able to easily come after me. I ran as fast as I could on the slippery ground, occasionally skidding or running into a root or branch.

The woods transitioned into a large cornfield, and I recognized it as the field belonging to Ezra Brouwer. Once I crossed through the cornfield, I would be back in the woods outside of the boundary of Sleepy Hollow, on the path to Tarry Town. The tall, dying corn stalks hid most of my movements, though it was difficult to know if I was running in a straight line. I batted scratchy leaves from my face as I followed one of the neat rows for what felt like hours. I finally pushed through the snowy field to find myself on a small stretch of bare ground, and, only a few paces away, the forest that ringed Sleepy Hollow. I made a dash across the open space and into the trees, my throat tightening excitedly in my chest. The path was so close, my bid for freedom successful!

But then I hit nothing at all and suddenly found myself flung to the ground.

I ended up in a heap, for I had been running at nearly full speed through the woods. My blanket fell away, my burlap sack of supplies went flying. Nothing was immediately in front of me. Trees surrounded me, and I could barely see the thin path that had led into Sleepy Hollow off to my right. I thought at first I must have slipped, or had hit an unseen branch, but after I collected my things and started forward, I was suddenly stopped again, as if a pane of glass lay in front of me, so clear I could not see it. I reached out a hand, and in the nothingness, my fingers flattened, as if the very air were a window. The Horseman's words rang in my ears. *Once you cross the line of magic into this glen, you become part of Sleepy Hollow, and you cannot leave. If you were to try, the magic would prevent you.*

I was not one for swearing, but I let out several words unbecoming of a schoolmaster under my breath as I groped my hands around the area. I crouched on the ground to feel along, then stood as high as I could reach. I even tried throwing my bag of provisions up and over what I hoped was only an invisible wall, but it only rebounded back down into my hands. I tracked along toward the east to see if it perhaps opened further away from the village, but it did not. No matter how far I walked, I could not move beyond the boundary of the magic that marked Sleepy Hollow for its own.

Despair caught in my chest like a fly in a spider's web. I might be well and truly trapped. I tried to picture what else was around me. I could cross to the other side of the path, with the forest by the wheat field, and try this same game of charades, looking for the edge of the wall that trapped me. But a little ways beyond the western half of the village lay the river. There was no way that I would be able to brave the icy, rushing rapids of the Hudson. To jump in there was tantamount to suicide. If I moved further inland, perhaps I could eventually find the edge of Sleepy Hollow's eastern border, where the magic might not stretch. It was not a great idea, but neither was throwing myself into the Hudson.

The sun was traveling downwards, as sunlight does so early in wintertime, and the trees were already starting to be cast in shadow around me. The wind whipped, and even the blanket about my shoulders did not protect me from the punishing cold. I could not stay out in the woods tonight, for I would surely freeze before the moon had even reached its zenith. I had precious few options available to me. The longer I remained outside, the more likely the villagers would be to spot me. I could find a barn or storehouse to hole up in for the night and resume my attempts in the morning, but the possibility of being spotted was even more likely then, and I could not even be sure I would find an escape. My brain told me that logically there had to be a way out, but I was not dealing with logic. I was dealing with magic, and magic made its own logic.

I stood, my feet planted in the snow, trying to decide what to do, when the excruciating pain struck. I doubled over, clapping a hand to my mouth to muffle the scream that came out of me as my body jerked and convulsed, the pain in my chest that of someone twisting a red-hot poker inside of it. My vision blurred, and tears froze in the corners of my eyes as I twitched and shook, chest heaving. The agony only lasted for a few moments, but each one felt like an eternity. I was sure I was in the pits of Hades itself. When the pain subsided and began to fade away, I realized I was lying on the ground, the blanket tangled around me. I unclenched my hand from my mouth, only to double over again as I retched uncontrollably.

What came out of me was not the meal I'd eaten, nor bile of any color, but a whisp of black smoke, not unlike that from a chimney. It collected into a mist under my shaking form before, with deliberate movements, it whisked away into the forest, lost amongst the trees. I could do nothing but stare after it, hazy and weak-kneed, lying on the bed of snow as if I had grown roots there.

I laid there for I knew not how long, but the light had faded further, the sun already sinking behind the trees. I had broken out into a sweat. The snow had felt good against my body after I had vomited whatever it was that had come from inside me, but now I was freezing again, my teeth chattering uncontrollably. I had to get up, or I really would die here. I had to get out of these woods, out of the cold. I did not know where to go, so I leaned heavily against the invisible border of Sleepy Hollow, getting to my knees, and then to my feet, chest heaving, limbs aching. Keeping my hand against the barrier, I stumbled along, not sure what direction I was going, but my mind was too fuzzy to care. I only knew I had to move.

The snap of a branch underfoot nearby made my head jerk up, and it took a moment to focus on the blurry outline of two figures approaching me at a leisurely pace through the dim light. When my mind finally managed to lock onto what it was seeing, my whole body went numb.

Katrina Van Tassel and Abraham Von Brunt stepped from around a nearby tree, only a dozen paces away from me. They were dressed in warm clothing and cloaks, and Brom carried a lantern. Katrina smiled at me, a sweet smile that was distorted by all of her teeth suddenly flashing with pointed ends. "Hello, Master Crane," she said pleasantly. "You seem to be lost."

I groped around me for any sort of weapon, but in my dizzy state and fear, I could find nothing but air.

Katrina removed her hand from her muff and held it out to me. I could see that her fingernails and fingertips had melded together into sharp, black points that seemed to be growing longer and sharper by the moment. "How strange that the Horseman decided to give me a challenge this year; that is very unlike him. Though it seems that you squandered that generosity."

I shrank back, my heart thundering in my chest and my ears. "What do you want from me?" I said, trying to sound demanding, but I knew it came out as no more than a croak.

Katrina giggled. "Do not worry, Ichabod. It will not take long, unless you want it to."

I turned and ran. I could barely see anything in front of me, crashing blindly through the trees for all of the world to hear. I took a sharp turn, bursting out of the trees and into the clear area in front of the fields. I was unsure where I was going but feeling only the sheer and utter need to get away. I skidded on a slick patch of ground, feeling my ankle twist, but I dared not stop, only sprinted forward to plunge into the cornfield.

I heard a sound behind me almost like the crunching of bone, and then there was something quadrupedal chasing after me. I could not tell what it was, but I could hear panting behind me, like that of a giant dog, and something else that sounded like a high-pitched screech. I continued to shove my way through the thick stalks. Each row looked the same as the last, and I had no destination in mind, only knowing that if I were to stop, I would die. I turned sharply, hoping to deter whatever was chasing me as I ran in another direction.

I could see trees up ahead. The forest was not far. I sprinted for it, until my foot caught a patch of ice, causing me to skid wildly. I hit the snowy ground, rattling my teeth in my skull, rolling a few feet. I turned onto my back, just as a large creature with a hideously smashed face and large fangs pounced on top of me. It looked like it was made of stone, except for the vicious, dripping mouth and glowing, red eyes that stared down at me. I screamed, feeling its weight baring down on me like a boulder. Its clawed fingertips dug into the soft flesh of my sides below my ribs, like icicles pricking my body. And then there was another cracking sound, and the creature above me morphed into Brom Bones, sitting triumphantly on my legs, fingers still dug into my tender skin.

"Gotcha," he said with a menacing smirk, not even breathing hard as he stared down at me with glinting eyes.

I shoved at him, but he was as immovable as a cornerstone. I looked past him to suddenly see Katrina descend from the sky a short distance away. Her black cloak and arms were spread wide, and I could see that they had morphed into a pair of leathery bat wings. She alighted upon the ground with a curl of black smoke not unlike that which had spewed forth from my body earlier, and her cloak settled back into position on her shoulders. Her blackened fingers were wickedly long and sharp now, almost like sickles. "What fun. You have given us a merry chase," she said, batting her eyelashes slightly. "But you have lost, Ichabod Crane, and now it is time to pay the price. The town will thank you for it. Posthumously, of course."

Brom yanked me up by my collar, then grabbed me by the top of my head to pull me to my knees. My life flashed before my eyes as Katrina stepped closer, drawing back her clawed hand to strike.

The roar of an angry horse sounded so close that I almost lost my hearing. Something struck Brom and sent him flying, ripping some of my hair from my scalp as he did. A large, black figure moved between me and Katrina. I looked up through bleary eyes to see the Horseman atop his fiery-eyed mount, as vicious and horrific as he had been on Halloween night when he chased me through the woods. Katrina stumbled backward. The Horseman reached out his hand to me, and without any other thought in my head, I took it. He yanked me up with supernatural strength, and the horse had started running before I had even thumped onto his back behind the Horseman.

Something screeched, something cracked, and my arms clung around the Horseman's waist with every bit of strength I had left in my body as the horse's hooves thundered through the corn. Within a few moments, we had cleared the field and were plunging back into the trees. I ducked my head low, pressing my forehead into the Horseman's back, clinging to him as though my very life depended on it, and I was sure in this moment that it did. The black horse expertly dodged trees and branches while the Horseman spurred him on, with only the rising moon above us to guide our way.

Wind whistled past me, and I finally pulled my face from the Horseman's coat to risk a glance over my shoulder. Nothing seemed to be pursing us, the forest deathly silent except for the canter of heavy hoofbeats. But I could not relax, and the Horseman's speed did not slow. He urged the great horse on, seeming to know exactly where he was heading. I started to hear running water nearby and realized we must be approaching the river that separated the church from the rest of the forest.

We suddenly hit the clear path, and I could see the bridge leading to the churchyard in the distance, drawing up fast. But I could also see on the path behind us that Brom was back in his monstrous creature form and lumbering after us on all fours like a great bear. Katrina was swooping above the trees with her giant wings, baring down on us. "Ichabod, let go of me and grab the back of the saddle," the Horseman said to me. My hands did not want to unclench from where they held him so tightly around the waist, but the urgency in his voice compelled me to release him and grab the saddle for dear life. Without further warning, the Horseman sprang off of the steed's back at a full gallop, into the path of the fanged Brom monster.

The horse continued its sprint, suddenly speeding up now that it only had one rider's weight upon it. It was only steps from the wooden bridge when I heard the dull thud of bodies colliding, and two screeches, one low and one higher. The horse hit the planks of the bridge, continuing its high speed rush until it burst out the other side in a parody of the chase that we had conducted on Halloween night. It started to slow, and I turned, trying to see what had become of the Horseman and our pursuers.

The Horseman was on the ground, the stone beast snorting and lashing at him as they scuffled. Above them, the giant bat screeched and tried to dive in to help. The Horseman struck at her, but, no matter how violent his movements, they halted inches from the bat before they could connect. She struck at him with her clawed feet, trying to drag him off of the gargoyle, but when he tried to grab at her claws, his hands would stop in mid-air before he could touch her. It almost seemed like he met the same resistance I had hit when I ran face-first into the barrier around Sleepy Hollow. Invisible, strong, relentless.

The bat backed off as the gargoyle was able to get the Horseman onto his back, snarling and snapping. The Horseman lifted his feet and front-kicked the monster sharply, directly into the bat. Both of them went flying and hit a nearby tree with a thunk that I felt all the way across the river. The Horseman stumbled to his feet and began to stagger toward the bridge.

The bat and the gargoyle were in a heap on the ground, and then Katrina and Brom were scrambling to their feet. I could already see something bright burning in Katrina's hand. I wanted to scream a warning to the Horseman, but I did not have any breath left in my lungs. The Horseman's boots had just touched the bridge when Katrina loosed a ball of fire straight for him.

It was as if the bridge too had the same magical barrier as the town, for the fireball struck the opening of the bridge right in front of the Horseman before it exploded into dozens of tiny sparks. The blast sent both the Horseman and witch and minion flying backward, the Horseman's body hitting the wooden planks of the bridge with a thump. The next thump was my own body hitting the snowy ground next to the black horse as I once again lost consciousness.

Chapter Five

I was not tied or gagged when I woke up this time. A lantern burned nearby, and when I was able to open my eyes to see my surroundings, I found that instead of the gallery, I was in the main area of the church. Blue moonlight poured through the glass windows, illuminating the space further. I realized that I had several blankets on top of me, which were keeping me surprisingly warm, especially once I realized with a start that I was naked underneath them. I sat up sharply, clutching the blankets to my chest.

The Horseman sat in the front pew a few feet away, and I realized I was on the raised dais, the pulpit stairs behind me. The Horseman's head was perched on the back of the pew as his body moved, and I realized that he was sewing something. He heard my movements and turned his eyes toward me. "We need to stop meeting this way." His face remained impassive, but his voice held a hint of mirth.

"I... I thought you had died," I said, remembering the ball of fire that had blown him backward on the bridge.

"I was dead to begin with," the Horseman said, a smile curving his lips upward. "I am almost done stitching up your clothes. Are you warm enough for now?"

I clutched the blankets closer, my cheeks warm with embarrassment as I realized that he must have undressed me while I was unconscious. "Yes," I said. Almost as an afterthought, I added, "Thank you."

The Horseman nodded and went back to his work. I cautiously lifted the blanket to examine myself, making sure I kept things hidden from him. I had cuts and scratches over my chest and sides, and my left ankle was swollen. But the wounds had been cleaned and dressed, and my ankle to bound with bandages.

The Horseman tied off the thread he had been using, then folded the garment and set it on top of the pile of my clothing at his side. He picked them up and crossed the few paces over to me, laying them down next to me before backing off again, his hands up in a show of truce. "Shall I leave you to get dressed?" he asked.

My whole body flushed at that. "Please."

The Horseman collected his head from the back of the pew, then turned and strode out through the side door. Once he was gone, I cautiously pushed the blankets aside and slid on my clothes. I could see repaired rips and gashes where the gargoyle had struck me, all neatly sewed back into place with fine stitches.

Once I had my clothing on, minus my jacket, for I was still feeling warm enough in just my shirtsleeves and waistcoat, I felt better and sat waiting for the Horseman to return, unsure what else to do. It was several more minutes before he cracked open the door and asked, "May I enter?"

"Yes," I said. He did, and I could see that the world was still shining white outside. He stomped off his boots, then padded over to me with a bucket of water, which he set down nearby before he retreated back to the pew, his head in his lap, and we sat in uncomfortable silence for a long while.

I opened my mouth to start to thank him when he also began to speak, and both of us lapsed into embarrassed silence again. I waved my hand at him to prompt him, and he coughed softly. "I hope your wounds are not hurting too badly."

"I am all right, thank you."

And then we fell quiet again before I finally said, "Thank you for saving me from the witch."

The Horseman looked up in surprise. "Was that all right?"

I laughed weakly. "It is not as if it can be undone if it was not. But... I am grateful. You did not have to do that."

The Horseman sighed and brushed some of his hair back behind his ear. "For anyone else, I might not have."

"Then why did you come to find me?" I asked.

He shrugged. "I do not know. There is something about you, Ichabod Crane. Something that draws me to you. And I decided I could not let you die out there, alone in the woods."

"I am glad you did not," I said softly, a warmth blooming in my chest at his words. He had risked his own safety to protect me, even after I had raised a tirade against him. "I am ready to believe you now."

The Horseman let out an unexpected chuckle at that. "Seeing is believing. I suppose I can hardly fault you for being skeptical. You seem like a man of logic and sense."

I snorted. "Apparently not enough sense to not run alone into the woods in the middle of winter."

"You were stressed," the Horseman soothed.

"I said some terrible things to you," I admitted.

"You did," the Horseman replied but said nothing more.

After another minute of silence, I cautiously rose to my feet, unsure if my ankle would take my weight, but with the help of the railing, I was able to step off the dais to stand in front of him. I found myself wondering if I was being rude by addressing his head only, from where it sat on his lap, which seemed a rather ridiculous thing to be considering, and hesitantly offered him my hand to shake. "I offer my sincerest apologies for the cruel things I said. I am grateful that you came to save me. Again."

The Horseman took my proffered hand and gave it a firm shake. "Consider it forgotten."

I hesitated, then gestured to the pew. "May I sit with you?"

In an instant, he had scooted over to give me room so we still had a respectable distance between us, his body turned slightly to face mine, and I did the same as I sat. "I am feeling more myself today."

"The curse was no doubt working upon your heightened emotions to try to drive you into the witch's path."

I shuddered, recalling the monstrous, stone form of Brom leaping onto me and the swirl of black mist as Katrina had alighted from the sky, transforming from a giant bat. "I am of more sound judgement now, I hope."

"I hope as well," the Horseman said, sounding like he might be trying to hide a smile.

I frowned slightly as I studied him. "Were you injured?"

"No," the Horseman said. "I am unharmed. Concern yourself not with me." He seemed to sense my hesitancy, because he said, "You may ask whatever you wish, and I shall answer."

I flushed at that and cleared my throat. "Oh. Well... I assume that you are... not amongst the living."

"Correct," the Horseman replied.

"But yet your person is... whole," I said, with a vague gesture to his body. "Un... blemished."

"I am a spirit," the Horseman said. "I am given this corporeal form, but it is not my true human body." I did not find this entirely unexpected, though I was surprised at how solid he felt for being a spirit rather than flesh and blood.

"Can you not reattach your head in your spirit form?" I asked.

"No," the Horseman said. He lifted his head up with his hands, and my relief was almost immediate as he set it to the empty space above his shoulders. And suddenly the being was a whole man. Long, black hair was tied back from a face that was pale, with an aquiline nose beneath mahogany-colored eyes and thick brows. It was a handsome face, I realized now, unsure why I had not seen it before, though I suspected that a head disembodied from its frame was likely not going to seem attractive no matter the circumstance. "I know approaching you with head in place would have been more prudent, but if I do not hold it, it will tumble, and I suspect that would be more frightful than simply appearing as I am."

That image was both absurd and disturbing. "I expect you are right," I said. At least with his head currently in its correct placement, I had a much better idea of the man I was speaking to. "Though that does not seem like a comfortable position to maintain."

He shook his head, while still holding it in place, and it was so odd to see that I nearly burst out laughing. But it felt like that would be impolite, so I only let out a single soft exhalation of fearful mirth. The thin lips curled into a smile that was not unkind, perhaps even a bit sheepish. I could see when he smiled that his right front tooth was just a bit crooked.

It seemed a rather cruel irony that the man was brought back as a spirit with his head still not attached to him after death, but I supposed that was less cruel than reviving his desecrated body from whatever place it currently resided. "How long have you been... not alive?" I asked. The question seemed rude, but of course, it was not as if I had experience making small talk with undead creatures.

"It has been a number of years," the Horseman said thoughtfully.

I swallowed hard, noticing the awkwardness of his position. "Please, do not hold your head up on my account."

"Are you certain?"

"Yes," I said.

His eyes met mine, and he gave me what seemed to be an apologetic smile before carefully lifting his head from its precarious spot above his shoulders and settling it once more onto his lap. The gesture of a man so calmly removing his own head from his body might have sent me into a fit of hysterics if I had not been anticipating it, and I was suddenly very glad he had approached me the first few times in his true form, which now at least seemed more natural, if not still slightly unsettling. What fragile creatures humans were, I realized in that moment.

"Would... Would you be gracious enough to tell me everything again, that I may better understand?" I asked, licking my lips nervously.

"Yes. I would tell you my story that connects it as well, if you would hear it," he offered. There was something in his voice that I thought might be hope. I wondered when his last opportunity to share his own story with anyone had been, so I settled back against the bench.

"Yes, please. I would like to hear it all."

And so the Horseman told me his story.

"I do not remember my parents or how I came to be on my own in this world, but I know I arrived in Sleepy Hollow as a young man, no older than you are now. I do not remember the year, only that it was long ago, before the town even existed as more than a few log cabins. I built my own house here, and the town began to emerge around me, growing with new people every day. This church we are sitting in was one of the structures I helped build. Families began to come, raise children, clear the area for farming. It was a charming place, the sort of place you might find in a fairy tale, with bright grass, perfect soil for planting, the river not far away. The sort of place where one might live happily for all of his days.

"And then the Van Tassels came. I do not remember how long I had been living in the town upon their arrival, but it had been a number of years. I was still a single man, for my desires lay outside of a woman and family, and I was busy with helping the town to prosper and thrive. There were three Van Tassels when they first came. Baltus Van Tassel, his wife, Elizabeth, and Baltus's daughter Katrina, who was well on her way to womanhood. They were kind and devoted to Sleepy Hollow. They built a grand estate, the very one you visited for the harvest party. They were very wealthy, though by what means, I could not say.

"They lived with us in peace in Sleepy Hollow for what must have been a year or so. And then Elizabeth became very sick and died within a fortnight. After her pious stepmother died, a change came over Katrina. She had seemed a sweet, demure lass, but after her stepmother was gone, she changed into something dark. Something evil. I do not know how long she had been practicing the dark arts of witchcraft.

"Things began to change in Sleepy Hollow, though it was subtle to begin with. The harvest that year was bountiful, the townspeople were rarely sick. The first sign that something nefarious was going on was the sudden arrival of a young, brutish man that had not ever been seen in these parts. He arrived in the night, the same night Elizabeth Van Tassel left this earth, and not a single person had seen him enter the town. He came from the direction of the Van Tassel estate with no idea of who he was or where he had come from. He was taken in by Master Van Brunt and his wife, both of whom were older and barren. He was given the name Abraham, though his nickname soon became Brom Bones. And he was very often seen at the side of Katrina, doing her every bidding, following her every missive.

"The year after Brom's arrival, the Van Tassels held a grand harvest party on Halloween night. The entire town attended, including myself. Every man, woman, and child in Sleepy Hollow was at the Van Tassel estate, drinking and carousing and dancing. As the sun sank and darkness fell, many people began to head home, for the forest was quite dark at night. I was intending to make my own exit when Katrina handed me what seemed to be a small goblet of wine. She said it was a new vintage she and her father were making and wondered if I might be willing to give my opinion before it was shared with the townsfolk. She had been a most gracious hostess, so I drank it without a second thought. Only minutes later, I was staggering as though I had drank an entire barrel of cider, and I fell into darkness.

"When I came to, we were outside, somewhere in the woods between the Van Tassel estate and the hollow. It was very dark, the moon overhead illuminating the branches above my head. I realized I had been tied to the ground by stakes driven into the earth, spread out like a five-pointed star, and I could not break the bonds that held me. There were torches in a circle around me, and nearby stood Brom Bones, Baltus Van Tassel, and Katrina.

"Katrina knelt beside me and told me that which I now relate to you. She and her father were witches who had evaded execution years before, though not before Katrina's birth mother had been hung for witchcraft. Baltus and his daughter had escaped and had been looking for a place to call their own. They had traveled for a long time, across the seas and back, during which Baltus found Elizabeth and married her. The three of them returned to the New World, and Baltus and Katrina decided that this place, Sleepy Hollow, was to be their safe haven. I suspect Katrina had started down the path of darkness sometime in those years, and it had awakened a violent desire inside of her. I do not think that Elizabeth Van Tassel was a witch, or that she knew she lay in the company of them. She had been a child of nature, a lover of life and goodness. I believe with all of my heart that they siphoned her soul from her for use in their magic. Her death gave Katrina and Baltus the power needed to create a minion of darkness, Brom Bones, and to seal their safe haven off from the world.

"Magic has a price that must always be paid. The price for life is death; not even such a powerful witch as Katrina could escape that terrible fact. The night of that first harvest party on Halloween night, I do not know why she chose me, of every person in Sleepy Hollow; I suspect it was simply that I did not have a family who would be seeking me out. She told me that I was to be the first blood sacrifice. Every year on Halloween, she would need to sacrifice someone to maintain her magic over the town. I was to become her scapegoat. The memory of me would be erased from the townspeople. They would not remember my name or that I had ever been their friend and neighbor. I was to become a specter, a spirit that would haunt these woods with my presence. She would blame me for the death of the annual sacrifice so she would not have to expend power on erasing the town's memory of their loved ones. She vowed that I would haunt these woods as a spirit as long as she was alive. And, with that, she then took an ax and struck my neck with supernatural force.

"When I returned to the land of the living, I was no longer of flesh and blood, but in this form you see now. My physical body was consumed by flame. She took my head, though I know not what she ever did with it. And then, I was abandoned here, in the woods. I stumbled upon this church in my despair, my memory of myself already fading, but I remembered how I had helped build it, though who had been with me was already forgotten. This hallowed space was built and consecrated before the Van Tassels moved to the area, and it became my safe haven. Neither the Van Tassels, nor Brom Bones, nor any of the villagers can cross the bridge into the churchyard without my permission. They know this is where I make my home, but they cannot reach me here. I could not, and still do not, remember much of my life before becoming a spirit. Those things I do remember, I have recounted to you in this tale. But I cannot leave Sleepy Hollow, in the same way you could not, nor can anyone else who enters the borders of these cursed lands. That which enters the hollow can never leave."

The Horseman fell silent after this recounting. I sat on the hard bench, utterly absorbed by his narrative, though my heart ached for his loss. "How long have you been here, alone?" I asked when it seemed that he had finished speaking and was waiting for my response.

"I do not know. Many, many years. Many, many sacrifices. Around a century, if I had to guess."

"How does the curse work?" I asked softly, morbid curiosity getting the better of me.

"At the harvest party, Katrina will place a hand on the chest of their intended victim and impregnates the spell into their heart," the Horseman said. "You probably felt it when she did."

I recalled the sharp pain under my ribs when Katrina had touched me during her flirtations to get me to stay with her and Brom. "Yes, I did," I said.

"Once they leave the party, Katrina and Brom pursue them through the forest. When they catch them, they decapitate them, as she nearly did to you in the field. Their soul is used to power her dark magic for another year."

"When I was hiding from the villagers, I heard them say that the Horseman usually only takes their heads, not their whole body," I said. "What actually happens?"

"She takes the head with her. I do not know what she does with them or if she even has them still in her possession. She leaves the body in the forest for the villagers to find."

A shudder ran through me, imaging Katrina scooping up my head from the ground after loosing it from my shoulders. "What do the villagers do with the bodies?"

"They burn them," the Horseman said solemnly. "They believe I have taken them and bestowed my own curse upon them, and fire is the only way to destroy that."

"But you have never killed any of them?" I asked.

The Horseman paused, and I jolted a bit. "You have?"

He sighed heavily, body folding over as if he were in pain. "Once, I did. One of the ones in the beginning. When I knew the curse would eventually kill. She was in so much pain. She did not have the courage to do it herself, so she pleaded with me to do it."

I felt a shudder wrack through me. How bad would the pain get? I had already lost myself to blackness multiple times from it.

The Horseman curled up on himself a little more as he said solemnly, "I understand if you cannot forgive me for that."

"What? For killing her?"

"Yes," he said, his voice nothing more than a whisper.

I frowned. "It is not I who would need to forgive you for that." As I watched him, the guilt tugged at me. "You do not forgive yourself for doing it?"

"I don't know," the Horseman said, his voice heavy. "I know it ended her suffering." His body straightened up so he could lift his head with his hands to meet my eyes. "But I know the way that you might suffer. It would have been more merciful of me to not have saved you."

I frowned at that, slowly reaching out one hand to lay it ever so gently on his leg. It felt solid and warm as any living human body. "I am glad you saved me," I said, brimming with truth. "Even if I am unsure why you did."

He was silent for a long moment before he rose to his feet. "I am going to walk the grounds. Stay here where it's warm, and rest."

And then he was striding away from me with powerful steps, out the door before I had much opportunity to formulate a protest.

I explored the church, which was quite small, but the Horseman had made it into a rather cozy sort of place. I inspected many of the figurines I found. Some of the tiny details were exquisite, especially for someone who was working without his head in the proper place. I wondered if perhaps that helped, being able to be closer to the work, though it was an odd question I was not about to ask.

I peered out the windows, able to see part of the churchyard with its gravestones through the rippled glass. I was not going to receive a burial. The villagers would torch my body after Katrina took my head. That was not a comforting thought.

When the Horseman returned, I asked him about the black steed he rode, since I had not seen it since I had fallen off of it on our return. "His name is Daredevil," he told me as he set down a handkerchief full of fruit for me to eat. "He does not reside here. He only appears at night, and when I have need of him, as if my desire conjures him. And both he and I can only leave this sacred ground once the sun has set. At daybreak, he will vanish."

I realized that was why the Horseman had come for me when he did after I had left in my impotent rage. He had had to wait for the sun to set before he could leave the safety of the churchyard. "What if you are out at daybreak?"

The Horseman chuckled sardonically. "I am transported back here, to this church. It is probably best that way. When I am not on hallowed ground, I am vulnerable to the witch. She and her minion are the only ones who can harm me."

"What about Baltus?" I asked curiously.

"His power is weak," the Horseman said. "He is barely a witch at all. Katrina's magic comes from her mother's side."

We sat in companionable silence while I ate the fruit. I offered some to him, but he refused. "I do not need to eat or sleep. But you do, so any food I have here is for you."

"Is it hard, to not do the human things you used to do?" I asked. I knew I would miss eating if I were not able to anymore.

"A little," the Horseman said thoughtfully. "I think it would not feel like such a loss if I were not alone with my own thoughts all of the time."

"I am often alone too," I said. "I mean, before all of this, of course. I thought I liked being alone. But I do not think I could bare the solitude you have faced."

The Horseman gave a little chuckle. I started to ask him another question, but I realized that in the entire time I had known him, he had not once mentioned his own name or that of his family. "What is your name?" I asked suddenly.

He blinked and stared at me with wide eyes. "My name?"

"Yes. Before you died."

He was silent for a long moment before he finally said, "It has been so long since anyone has asked me that."

I noticed he did not answer the question. "Do you not remember?" I asked in surprise.

He gave a small shake of his head. "No. I think, when Katrina cursed me to be forgotten by the townspeople, she erased my name too."

"So you do not even recall your own name?" I said, aghast.

"No," he said gravely. Something flared in me, hot and sad. This man had had his life cut brutally short, living a lonely, exiled life in the woods of Sleepy Hollow, and he could not even remember who he was before that happened to him. "I'm sorry," I said.

His dark eyes met mine, giving me a small smile. "Thank you."

"I... What shall I call you?"

"Everyone calls me the Horseman."

Another bit of sadness swirled in my stomach. "But that is not really who you are," I said. "Everyone should have a name."

He blinked. "You really are remarkable, Ichabod Crane."

"See? You know my name," I said, and his eyes sparked with amusement. "Your horse has a name. You should have a name."

"Will you choose one for me?" the Horseman asked.

"Choose a name for you?" I echoed.

"Yes."

That surprised me, for the Horseman was a man, not a dog or even a child. "Do you not wish to choose your own?"

He shook his head where it rested on his lap. “It has been so long since I have been out in the world. It would mean more to me if you were to select one for me.”

My mouth went dry at that, and I cleared my throat. “Really?”

“Yes. You have been so kind to me in what must be a time of great terror for you. I would be honored for you to choose what to call me.”

Every name I had ever known suddenly went out of my head, and I stared at him for a long moment. What did one call a headless specter who haunted the woods on Halloween after being cursed by a witch? A simple name would probably be best, but this man was hardly simple. And then it came to me, landing in my mind like a bird settling upon its nest. “Reiter,” I said. His head cocked curiously. “Your accent is Germanic. Reiter is German for ‘Rider.’” Perhaps that was a bit on the nose, but the Horseman scrunched up his face thoughtfully before smiling.

“Reiter. I like that.”

At least I had not displeased him. My heart gave a little flip-flop at the smile on his face, glad that I now had a name to connect to the fearsome Horseman of Sleepy Hollow.

Chapter Six

After that, Reiter and I had a much easier relationship. He would go out at night, into the woods behind the church, or sometimes over the bridge, to hunt food for me, or sneak into the village to take from their storehouses. I did not like when he was gone, for I could not know if he was safe or if I might suddenly be left alone. But he was always back before the sun rose, bringing all manner of game, forest fruits and vegetables, and even cheese from the storehouses. One night he even brought an entire apple pie that he had taken off a windowsill. I rather hoped the owner of the home had not seen the Headless Horseman of Sleepy Hollow sneaking around stealing pastries off of window ledges, of all things.

There was plenty of fresh water from the well in the back or from the stream over which the bridge flowed, and wood from the forest to keep the church warm, cook food, and heat water for me to bathe. Reiter did not need to sleep, and the temperature did not affect him; the nest of blankets he had laid me on the first night of my arrival was simply a place he liked to sit and read, and it became my private space where I might sleep or be alone. When I asked if the grand pipe organ worked, he said that it did but that he did not often play. His own skills on the keys were completely self-taught. "Would you like me to teach you?" I offered, my own fingers itching to get back to music again.

"I would like that," he agreed. So I sat on the old, wooden bench, and he perched next to me, holding his head up so he could see my hands moving over the keys, then moving his head, but not his body, down to watch my feet move the pedals. "It seems complicated," he said with a chuckle.

I opened my mouth to respond when a red-hot flare of pain burst in my chest, my heart pulsing like it was trying to break through my ribs. I screamed, my hands clutched to the spot as my body crumpled off the bench, and I hit the floor with a dull thump. My blood rushed in my ears, so loud I could not even hear myself. The agony twisted inside of me, as if my heart were trying to tear itself free of the sinew that attached it to me. I broke out instantly in sweat, and everything went black.

I thought it only lasted for a few seconds. When I opened my eyes, Reiter was kneeling next to me, his hands resting firmly on my arm. "Breathe," I heard him say, and I sucked in oxygen like a man breaking the surface of a churning ocean. The tension in my chest was starting to ebb a little, and, after a moment, I tried to push myself up, but my arms were shaking too much. I suddenly felt his strong chest press against me from behind as he held me close and helped me sit up, propping me up with his own body. I forced my lungs to work as I gratefully leaned against him, glad I did not have to support my own weight, limp as a rag doll.

A moment later, he was using the hem of his coat to wipe the sweat from my forehead. I froze in surprise at the gesture, so kind and comforting, something I had not experienced in the many years since my mother had passed away.

"Enough music for today," he said, helping me to my feet and smoothing back my auburn hair. "You look a little pale. Would you like to go for a walk in the churchyard? There is no snow on the ground currently."

I had yet to be outside of the church walls in my time here since my return, and the thought of fresh air, even if it was cold, invigorated my soul. "Yes. If it is safe."

Reiter nodded. "No one from Sleepy Hollow can cross the bridge or the river to this area, nor can I be seen by human eyes during the daytime. It is quite safe."

"Then I would love to," I said. We went down from the gallery, and he gave me a warm blanket to wrap around my shoulders before pushing open the door and leading me out into the churchyard, dotted with headstones.

The first few breaths chilled my lungs, but the coolness of the air, the nearby splash of water from the stream, and the murmur of birds overhead were a balm to my beaten soul. We walked along amongst the tombs, pausing once in a while for Reiter to point out one in particular. "I do not remember any of these people," he said. "They would have been from before I was cursed. But I will sometimes make up stories about who they were and how they knew me."

Sorrow flared in my chest at that. "You really can remember nothing from your life before that night at the harvest party?"

"Very little," Reiter said.

"Is that strange, to not know who you are?"

He was silent for a moment before he said, "It is, but I think after all of this time, I have come to accept that my former self is gone. If I had lived a normal life, I would have died by now, after over a hundred years. And no one can remember me. The witch wiped me from the face of this earth."

I frowned deeply. "No one outside of here may remember you, but for the time I have known you, you have been a true gentleman and friend. My time might be limited, but I cannot express how grateful I am to you for the comfort that has brought me."

Reiter sniffed, and I was startled to see the barest hint of tears forming in his dark eyes. "What is it?" I asked.

Reiter smiled sadly. "You are amazing, Ichabod Crane. You have made me feel something I have not felt in a very long time."

My naïveté got the best of me, and I cocked my head curiously. "What is that?"

Reiter shook his head. "No. I will not tarnish our friendship by naming what cannot be."

"Why can't it be?" I asked. "What is it?"

"No," Reiter said again, his eyes on the ground as we walked.

"Tell me," I insisted. "I am going to die anyway."

"You would think badly of me," he said.

I frowned. "I do not think that is possible."

Reiter hesitated before slowly lifting his eyes to meet mine. "I have feelings for you. More than simple friendship."

My brows furrowed as I tried to parse out the meaning of his words. "What sort of feelings?"

I heard Reiter audibly swallow before he said, "I think... I am beginning to love you."

The words struck me as if I had suddenly been punched, my heartbeat quickening in my chest. "You what?"

"I love you," Reiter said again, more forceful this time. "I love you, Ichabod, and I don't want to lose you."

My mouth suddenly went very dry. "Do you always feel that way about the sacrifices?" I asked. Reiter had known dozens of people in his time trapped in Sleepy Hollow, and there certainly was nothing unique about me.

"No," he said. "I have never felt this way toward any of them. But the first time I saw you, I knew that you were special."

I flushed at that, my fingers curling around the blanket about my shoulders. "Certainly not."

Reiter frowned. "Do you not believe that you could be special?"

I tried to swallow, but my mouth still felt as dry and heavy as sand. "No one has ever said they loved me before."

Reiter's gaze turned very sad. "Not ever?"

"No."

Reiter looked like that caused him physical pain. He was quiet for a moment before he ventured, "I notice that you did not seem repulsed by my statement."

I blinked. "I... I'm not," I said, slightly surprised at myself. It was true that Brom's crude proposal had repulsed me, but I had never thought that it was because he was a man, merely his brutish and lascivious nature.

Reiter stared at me for a moment. "Do you enjoy the... company of men?"

The question brought heat to my cheeks as I understood that he did not mean mere socializing, but something much more intimate. "I have never been with a man. Or a woman," I added, lest he think that my proclivities were only toward the fairer sex.

Reiter blinked, his head cocking so far to the side that he nearly dislodged himself from his own grip. "No?"

"No."

"Are you particularly religious?"

I laughed at that. "Good heavens, no. I grew up with religion, as most people do, but I could not say that I am very religious myself."

"Then, may I ask why you have not experienced the pleasures of the flesh?" His tone left room for me to deny his request if I wanted, but it wasn't as if there was anyone he would talk to about me.

"I suppose I have just never really felt the desire for it," I said. "Not found the right person. Though, I suppose, I will not get the opportunity."

His face fell just a bit, and I suddenly realized my thoughtless words. "No, I mean... Not that you are not the right person. You could be, I do not really know. I just meant that, if I am to die, I would not have the time to look beyond... you..." My voice trailed off as I realized how completely heartless I must sound.

Reiter's face was gentle. "I understand," he said. "I would not ever wish to make you uncomfortable or do something you did not wish to do. If I have offended you or disturbed you in any way, I offer my sincerest apologies and will never mention it again."

"No!" The exclamation came out of me before I had even thought it. I blushed and ducked my head a little. "I mean, that is... I am... flattered?" I wasn't sure if that was the word I was searching for, my loquacious vocabulary suddenly failing me.

"Are you?" he asked.

"I believe I am. It is simply entirely new to me to feel this way."

Reiter gave me a smile that sent a shiver down my back. "You are amazing, even if you do not realize it about yourself."

I flushed again. "Surely not."

"Ichabod. While I admit that my interactions have been limited for a number of years, I have not forgotten what humans are like. And I have not met one as clever and kind as you, either before or after my death."

I licked my lips with the tip of my tongue, and it did not escape my notice that his eyes tracked the movement. "How can that be? I am a simple man."

"Not to me," Reiter said. Something in my chest felt warm as I gazed back at him.

"I am not saying no," I ventured. "It is simply a lot to process on top of my precarious position."

"I understand," Reiter said again. "Take all of the time you need. If you do not return my feelings, I will not be offended or put out. I know that my own situation is hardly a favorable one." We had circled back to the door of the church now, and he held it open for me to enter. I moved over to the fireplace to warm my hands, and he tossed several more pieces of wood onto it to build it up for me as I settled in front of it.

"When you were... alive, did you... keep the company of men?" I asked as he sat a few feet away. The question felt rude to ask, but my curiosity was getting the better of me, to learn more about this man, his lonely existence, and anything that he might remember from his life before his tragic curse.

Reiter smiled at that. "Yes," he said. "Though, as far as I can remember, there was no one for whom I felt any sort of desire for a relationship. And, of course, the religious fervor made it difficult to find those willing to take the risk."

I frowned thoughtfully as I pulled off my shoes to warm my feet. It was only the two of us here; no one would be able to enter the church and disturb us. We were free to discuss it as much as we liked. "I am sorry you had to endure such hatred. I know that love is not easy to find."

"Is that sort of relationship more acceptable out there now?" he asked me curiously.

I sighed. "Not really. Some people don't mind, but the religious leaders are still quite against it."

Reiter laughed at that. "Of course, they are. But it is not like any of them helped me when I needed it either." He sobered again, gazing solemnly at me with his dark brown eyes. "I have flustered you enough, but what are your feelings about love?"

I ran my hand through my hair as I thought about my answer. "I admit that I have never been much of a romantic. But if two people find each other and bring each other happiness, I wish every good thing upon them. We all deserve a little happiness in this world."

Reiter's mouth quirked a bit. "We do."

I hesitated for a moment. The path ahead of me was so uncertain. Well, I realized, it was actually quite certain at this moment. I was going to die in the not-very-distant future. I felt something fluttering inside of me, though it was unfamiliar. "May I kiss you?" I asked Reiter before my nerves could get the better of me.

He blinked in surprise at that. "You wish to?"

I nodded. "I have not experienced it before. Perhaps it will give me further insight into my feelings."

Reiter was silent for a moment before he said, "I would like it very much if you kissed me."

"I do not promise anything more than that," I warned.

He gave a soft chuckle. "I do not expect anything more."

I smiled at that. He was not the monster of Sleepy Hollow. He was more the gentleman than any I had met in my travels. I looked over him, my lips curving into a frown as I registered the odd predicament. "How should I do it?" I asked, giving a vague wave of my hand at his disarticulated form.

Reiter coughed softly, his cheeks turning delightfully red. "Shall I hold my head in place?"

"That isn't comfortable for you," I pointed out.

"This is about you, not I," he said.

I felt my own cheeks warm, and then heat further as I decided that if I was going to do this, I was going to show him my level of comfort with his form. "May I hold your head?"

He blinked, and I wondered if perhaps I had offended him, before he said, "If you would like. I know it is rather unnerving."

"The whole situation is unnerving," I said, as lightly as I could. "You are hardly the most disturbing part of it."

"Once again, you amaze me, Ichabod," Reiter said.

"Will I hurt you?" I asked, suddenly wondering if I was asking too much to take his head from him. It was not as if I, or most anyone, ever had a reason to ask such a question.

"No," Reiter soothed before his hands lifted, and he held out his head to me, as if presenting a priceless gem. His eyes focused on mine, his thin lips curled into a reassuring smile.

I received his head into my hands, cradling it lightly with my fingers on either side of his jaw, trying to hold it for the precious vessel it was. It was oddly heavy, but I was careful not to press my fingers into his skin or bones, though I suspected I would not do any damage even if I did. I lifted him until his dark eyes were even with mine. His tongue slid out to brush his upper lip nervously, which for some reason made my heart flutter a bit in my chest. How could a man so terrifying and confident be so uncertain over something so simple? "Is this all right?" I asked.

"Yes," he said, and I was oddly glad he did not try to nod while I held him, for holding his head with nothing attached to it was an extraordinarily odd feeling as it was, never mind extraneous movement. His body remained still where he sat a few feet away, fingers curled into the knees of his trousers, as if to keep from reaching for me.

I slowly leaned in, his eyes watching mine, and I carefully pressed my mouth to his in the first kiss I had bestowed upon anyone's lips. It was not a good kiss, holding his face uncertainly, my mouth inexperienced in the pressure and the angle, but it was a kiss, nonetheless. When I pulled back from him, he blinked at me with those dark eyes and then smiled softly. "Was that strange?"

I laughed at that. "A little, but it is not as though I have done that with anyone else, so I do not have much of a comparison."

Reiter laughed at that too, the vibrations of it barely discernable on my palms. "I suppose that to be true."

"Is it strange for you?" I asked curiously.

Reiter's shoulders on his body shrugged nonchalantly, but there was something in the press of his lips together and the slight wrinkle between his eyes that betrayed his eagerness. "I have not kissed anyone while I have been in this form. It is a little strange. But not unpleasant."

"I am glad to know that I am not an unpleasant companion," I said with a chuckle.

"You can do it again if you'd like," Reiter said.

I raised a brow. "Would *you* like that?"

It seemed like he was trying to not show his enthusiasm as he simply replied, "Yes."

So I kissed him. It was still awkward and clumsy, but he did not seem to care, his lips pressing eagerly to mine. His eyes slid closed, and I mimicked him, backing off a little for him to take control of the kiss. It was warm and firm. His tongue suddenly brushed over my lips, and I jumped, pulling him back from my face. He blanched. "I'm sorry."

"No, I..." I brushed my own tongue over my lower lip. "I just was not expecting that."

"I will not do it if you don't like it."

"I was too surprised to know if I liked it," I said, giving him a smile. I drew him close to me again, pressing my mouth lightly to his. He kissed me back before opening his mouth against mine and brushing his tongue delicately across my lower lip. My lips parted, and his tongue drifted into my mouth. It was strange, though not unpleasant. But he moaned softly, and that sound sent a shiver of pleasure through me that I had not expected. He must have felt it, because he did it again, and I was glad I was sitting down, because my legs gave a slight tremble.

He finally moved a little to pull back, and I cradled his head lightly between my hands. "You liked that?"

I felt my cheeks heat again. "It was enjoyable enough."

He tipped his head slightly in my hands, which felt disconcerting. "But?"

"I liked the sounds you were making more," I confessed.

His brown eyes went wide, and he chuckled. "Oh, really?"

I gave him a shy smile. "Is that strange?"

"No," Reiter said, giving his head a small shake in my grip. "You seem to be attuned to sound, so it would make sense."

That made me laugh, and I leaned in to give him a quick peck on the lips. "You already know me so well."

His grin turned lascivious. "I would like to know you even more."

"What do you want to know about me?" I asked. He stared for a moment before his eyes flicked down to the front of my trousers. I blushed when his meaning became clear. "Oh. I... am not sure I am ready for that."

"That is all right," Reiter reassured me. "And if you never are, that is all right too. I would never force you to do something you did not want to do."

Unexpected tears heated my eyes at that. How was this man so kind after the many years of loneliness and anger he must have felt? "You are a truly good person."

Reiter frowned as he saw the tears welling in my eyes. "Ichabod," he soothed, and my name on his lips sent another unfamiliar shiver down my spine. "May I hold you?" he asked.

I blinked, the tears abating as I stared at him. "Hold me?"

"Yes." His body stirred a little, and I realized with a start I had forgotten about it, despite it only being a few feet away.

I swallowed hard and nodded. His body got up, and my heartbeat quickened just a bit as his headless form came to sit by me and wrap his arms around me. I cradled his head to my chest, leaning my own head lightly into his embrace. He stroked his hand down my arm but otherwise held still, just letting me relax into his touch. It had been so long since anyone had held me this close, I couldn't even remember it. And it certainly would not have been in a romantic way. Reiter's embrace was not flirtatious or demanding though, just holding me to his warmth. I sighed. "I could fall asleep like this."

"Go ahead," Reiter offered. I turned to look down at his head in my arms in surprise. He smiled back. "You know you are safe here. If you wish to sleep, sleep."

I hesitated, then cautiously placed his head next to his body on the ground. "So I don't drop you if I do."

He laughed. "Very thoughtful of you."

I nestled against his chest, resting my head over where his heart lay silent. And eventually, I did sleep.

Chapter Seven

The next morning, I washed with the bucket of water Reiter provided for me and ate an easy meal of cheese and fruit, and then I sat in the gallery and played the pipe organ. Reiter sat nearby, listening, his body swaying in time to the music. When I began to sing, his eyes closed, and he looked so at peace that I was determined to go through every song I knew in my repertoire for him, which took nearly the entire day. My voice was almost as hoarse as his when I finally stopped. "Thank you," he said when I had finished. I gave him a flourishing bow from the bench before I got up and moved to sit by him. I hesitantly lifted his head up to give it a soft, exploratory kiss, which he eagerly returned. My energy was flagging though, and he did not protest when I returned his head to his lap.

I rolled my shoulders and neck, for sitting on a bench all day was never good for one's posture, and I jumped when his hands landed on my shoulders and began to knead them. His large, strong hands moved over my tight muscles, thumbs digging into the knots and working them carefully. I was not used to this much touching, but his hands on me made my skin tingle in a way that I found surprisingly pleasant.

"Tell me what you know about the curse," I said suddenly, and his hands stilled for a moment.

"What?"

"What do you know of Katrina's magic? Her father's? When you fought her at the bridge, it seemed like you could not land a blow on her."

His hands began to move on my neck again. "That part is true. After she killed me, she took my head away with her. She does that for all of her victims, but I am the only one she hath resurrected. I think she has my skull, and because of that, I cannot harm her in any way."

"But she can harm you," I observed.

"Yes," he said. "Though we so rarely ever engage. That evening when I came to your aid was the first time we have done more than see each other in probably half a century."

I pondered that for a moment. "Do you think if your skull were returned to you, you would have the ability to cause her harm?"

"I would believe it so," the Horseman said thoughtfully. "She does not age or become ill, but neither is she fully immortal. I have seen her injured before, as have I seen the same of Baltus and Brom. I would think her susceptible to catastrophe the same as any mortal."

"Have you ever looked for your skull?" I asked curiously.

He actually laughed at that. "I have. I have searched the woods and the town, with no luck. The place I have not searched is their house and property."

I thought it very likely that the Van Tassels would keep something as precious as the Horseman's skull close to them. He was restricted to searching at night, but I was not. "I will help you find it," I said firmly. "We will learn what we can about her magic, and then we will find a way to defeat her."

Reiter stared at me. "Ichabod, you cannot possibly do such a thing."

"Why not?" I demanded. "I am dead if I do nothing. Why should I not help you?"

"It is a fool's errand," Reiter said.

I shrugged. "I need to plan anyway. I promise I will not rush out or do anything without telling you."

Reiter seemed uncertain at that, but he let the matter drop.

The next morning, we traded a few kisses, and Reiter massaged my shoulders and neck again with his strong, calloused hands. I was starting to very much enjoy touching, though I suspected it was because it was him. Eventually, Reiter stopped, and we spent some time reading silently, which still amused me to no end to see him hold the book on his lap with his head near it, his hands turning the pages.

I did not know how long it had been before I shifted to lean against his shoulder. "Are you nervous?" I asked.

"About what?" Reiter asked, closing his book and setting it aside, as if I was the most important thing in the world right now.

"If I were to go look for your skull at the Van Tassel estate."

He was silent for a moment before he replied, "I am not nervous for myself."

"Then what is it?" I asked.

"I am nervous that I might lose you. I could even say I was afraid."

I started a bit at that. "You are afraid you might lose me?"

"Yes," Reiter said. His fingers reached up to trail down my cheek gently. "I love you, Ichabod Crane. I am certain of it now. I know that is perhaps not fair of me to say, considering both of our circumstances, but I feel I should be honest with you."

I swallowed hard. While his confession was not surprising, considering our conversation not long ago, it suddenly felt like a large responsibility had been placed on my shoulders. For what, though, I could not tell.

Reiter's eyes turned toward the ground. "I apologize if that puts you in an awkward position. I do not expect you to love me back."

"Reiter," I said, and his gaze met mine again. "I... Please do not mistake my silence for rejection. I simply am... overwhelmed by all of these new feelings."

Reiter smiled weakly. "I am sure that your feelings, coupled to the precarious situation you are in, are rather distressing."

I hesitated. "I am not sure what I am feeling," I admitted. "Had we met in different circumstances, before this curse upon both of us, I believe that I would have relished a companion such as you.

But I do not know that I would ever have acted on any feelings, due to the nature of the world, and my own trepidations."

Reiter reached up a hand to cup my cheek. "There is no one else here but me," he said, his palm warm against my face before his fingertips glided down my jaw to my throat.

I inhaled softly. What if I died in the coming days? I had never considered myself to be a romantic, but death was a very real possibility. And if I was gone, Reiter would once again be alone, blamed for the attacks on the villagers. "Reiter," I said, reaching up to catch his hand, entwining our fingers together. "You are afraid of losing me. I would not wish to break your heart if that were to happen."

Reiter smiled sadly. "My heart would still be broken, even if you dropped dead this very moment."

That made me draw in a gasp of air. "I do not wish to hurt you."

"I know," Reiter said. "And I wish to protect you. I know that may damn me to an eternity of misery, but if this is the time we have together, I will treasure it, even if you want nothing more to do with me."

I immediately pulled him into my arms. "You did not abandon me in my hour of need, and I will not leave you to tread this darkness alone." I pressed my cheek to his shoulder, resting it there. "But if this all the time I have left, I would spend it with you."

His hand not holding his head rested in the center of my back, stroking up and down soothingly. "I would like that."

We were silent in each other's embrace for a few minutes before I asked, "Would you... show me what I have been missing?"

Reiter blinked, lifting his head up so he was eye level with me. "What?"

My face was hot as I replied, "If I am not to have a future, I believe I would like to experience-" what was the name bestowed by zealous preachers? "-carnal desire."

Reiter stiffened for a moment, then relaxed again, a soft smile playing over his lips. "If you wish it."

I cleared my throat uneasily. "Do not think me entirely naïve. I know how… that… happens. I am just unsure if I am ready for it."

Reiter brushed his hand lightly over my shoulder. "There are many ways to be intimate without *that*. Shall I show you?"

My cheeks flushed hot. "I would like that."

"You only have to tell me if you wish to stop," Reiter said, leaning in and lifting his head to my lips to press a kiss to them. "I would not ever want you to be scared or uncomfortable with me."

"You are such a gentleman," I said, my voice teasing to try to hide the nervousness that fluttered in my stomach.

Reiter laughed and kissed me again before pulling back. "We can start slowly. We do not even have to undress fully, if that would be more comfortable for you."

I blinked in surprise at the offering. "I think I would appreciate that for now. I am a little nervous."

"I know," Reiter said with a positively wicked grin. "You are as tight as a fiddle string under my touch."

His words made me laugh, and I felt the tension release from my shoulders, realizing they had been up around my ears. "Then you should play me," I said, trying to make my tone teasing, though I was not entirely sure I succeeded or that my joke even made sense.

Reiter gave me another kiss before setting his head down next to us. My eyes followed it until his hands closed on my shoulders, drawing me a little closer to him. His hands trailed up and down my chest, ever so gently, until one hand stopped to give the pebble of my nipple a light squeeze through the layers of fabric. I inhaled at the new sensation. He chuckled at me from the floor. "All right?"

"Yes," I said. "Do it again?"

His thumb brushed over the nub once more before his other hand grasped my other one and gave it a pinch, slightly harder than he had the first one. Heat shot through my body, down my spine, to low in my belly. He rubbed his thumbs over both of them, circling them through my shirt and waistcoat. A soft sound escaped my lips, a muffled whimper. He squeezed the spots again before running the pad of his thumb soothingly over them. "I could do more to them if you take off your outer layers."

I blushed, but I moved to slide my open jacket off my shoulders, letting it drop behind me. As my fingers worked at the buttons on my waistcoat, I gazed back at him. "Should I be...?" My voice trailed off, waving a hand vaguely at his own torso.

Reiter tensed for a moment, his hands resting on his thighs. "No. Let me pleasure you. I just want you to focus on relaxing."

I knew that was going to be difficult, but I nodded, shucking the vest off behind me as well. "Will you not reveal yourself to me?" I asked, reaching up to stroke my fingers over the shoulders of his jacket.

"I would not wish to disturb you more than I already do," Reiter said, his fingertips trailing down my face.

"You do not disturb me," I said, though I was grateful for the kindness of his tone and sensitivity of my feelings.

His headless shoulders hunched just a bit. "If it does not displease you, I would rather you not see me that way."

I blinked in surprise. It had not occurred to me that a spirit, much less one of a man so otherwise confident and capable, would have reservations about their own form, especially since it was not within his control. I supposed his vulnerability might feel equal to my own in that sense, his concern of rejection or other feelings of disgust. I ran my hand down the center of his chest. "It does not displease me," I said. "Your comfort is no less important. But know that I hold no animosity toward your form."

I could see the tension release from his shoulders then, and his hand stroked my cheek again. "You are truly a man of many surprises, Ichabod Crane. Perhaps one day I will feel that I may expose my whole form to you." His palm traced lovingly down my throat, and I briefly closed my eyes at the kindness in the touch. "Lie down," he purred, his voice deeper than it usually was. I blushed but shifted to carefully stretch out on the raised planks of the church podium, bunching my jacket under my head for a little softness.

Reiter knelt with his knees on either side of my hips, his trousers pressing just barely against mine as his hands slid up to toy with my nipples through my thin, linen shirt. His hands were strong against me, and I reveled in the unfamiliar, warm touch. It still was so new to me to have hands upon me in an intimate way, not just my students who sometimes wanted hugs or to hang off me like a tree swing. But I was starting to realize why people enjoyed hugging and caressing one another.

He twisted one of my nipples, and my hips jerked up of their own accord, the front of my trousers growing heavier as my blood rushed inside of me. Reiter chuckled, and rubbed his hips lightly back against mine. The front of his own trousers was tented with a large bulge. I blushed slightly at that. He smirked and trailed his fingers down the center of my chest. "What?" he purred.

I let out a nervous laugh that sounded more like a squeak. "I, uh, I have not... ever been the source of someone's desire before." Brom hadn't counted. Brom Bones would have molested a knot in a tree if he could reach it.

Reiter's hand paused in its movements, and he smiled softly at me. "I wanted you the moment I first laid eyes on you."

"When was that, exactly?" I asked, rolling onto my side so I could address his head properly.

Reiter actually blushed, which I found quite endearing. "One of your first nights in the village. I watched you from the woods as you dined with the de Viers."

I blinked in surprise, for that had been the first family I had stayed with in Sleepy Hollow. "You were watching me that early?"

"Yes," Reiter said, shifting his body to sit on the ground. I felt slightly apologetic for putting our explorations on hold, but this was a new part of the story that Reiter had not told me before.

"Did Katrina know you wanted me?" I asked, guilt tugging at my heart for thinking that Reiter might be the reason I had been chosen at the harvest party.

"No," Reiter said firmly. "I am certain she knows now, since I chased you to safety when she was after you, and I so rarely do that. But I knew that you would be the sacrifice this year. If there is a newcomer to the town, they are always selected."

I swallowed hard. "What if there is no one new?"

Reiter's eyes dropped to the ground. "Then one of the villagers is chosen. I do not know how she selects them. I believe it to simply be at her whim."

I sat up in surprise. "One of the villagers? And they don't become suspicious of her because she blames it on you?"

"Yes," Reiter said, sounding more than a little sorrowful.

I frowned, feeling heat behind my eyes. My heart suddenly gave a powerful beat in my breast, and I gasped, clutching my hand to it. In an instant, Reiter's hand was over mine, pressing lightly. "Breathe," he soothed. I exhaled sharply and tried to inhale again. These smaller surges in my chest were becoming more frequent now, and my stomach twisted to think what that might mean. A few deep breaths later, and the pain had faded completely, but Reiter's hand still held mine. "Are you all right now?"

"Yes," I said. "Thank you."

Reiter pulled back from me. "I suppose we shall stop what we were doing then."

I blinked in surprise. "I'm sorry, did I put you off?"

"No," Reiter said quickly, his head jerking in a shake on the floor. "But I probably have done so for you."

"No," I said. "I want to keep going, if you are willing."

Reiter smiled, and his body sat up and slid over mine again. "Very willing."

The lump in his trousers had lessened, as had my own, but he started to rub up against me, and I could feel the passion building inside of me once more. His fingers slid down to grasp one of my nipples through my shirt and gave it a light squeeze. I moaned as heat once again flooded my veins, arcing out from that tiny nub. He rolled it between his fingers, and I gasped, my hips rocking upward so we suddenly ground against one another. Next to me, I heard him groan. My thoughts wandered to if it was disconcerting for him to watch his own body and feel its pleasure while not being attached to it. But then he thumbed my other nipple and gave it a sharp tweak, and my mind snapped back to the large, firm frame against mine. He was so warm, as warm as any human would be, and I realized that I liked being under him this way. I felt secure and protected.

One of Reiter's hands slowly slid down my chest, down my stomach, and I inhaled as he brushed over the waist of my trousers. His fingers paused in their slide. "Is this all right?" he asked, just a hint of concern in his voice.

"Yes," I said, turning to give him a reassuring smile. "I will tell you if I want to stop."

Reiter smiled at me, and I couldn't resist leaning over to give him a kiss before settling onto my back again. His fingers dipped briefly just inside my trousers before he pulled his hand back again. I was about to open my mouth in protest when his hand suddenly palmed the front of my breeches, giving me a warm, gentle squeeze. I gasped, my hips arching upward toward his touch. He squeezed me again, and delicious fire welled in my belly.

"Does that feel good?" he asked, and I nodded, licking my lips nervously.

His hand rubbed up and down the front of my trousers for a moment, each brush of his fingers drawing my attention. I moaned a little louder, then flushed, pressing my lips together.

Reiter laughed. "No one will hear you, Ichabod," he soothed. "You may be as loud as you wish." He gave me a devilish grin next to me. "I like hearing your voice."

That made me blush like a school maiden again. But I realized that since I was letting him pleasure me without returning the favor, I could at least let him hear my appreciation. His hand stroked up and down for a minute, and my hips jerked as I writhed under him, gasping each time his hand slid back up.

"May I undo these?" he asked, motioning to the lacing that held my trousers in place.

"Yes," I breathed. His fingers made quick work of the laces, loosening them, and then using both hands to slide them down over my hips, just enough for my cock to spring free. I felt my whole body flush. Other than my mother when I was a child, no one else had seen this part of me, and my hands twitched to cover myself. I fought the desire and instead raised my hands over my head, gripping my makeshift pillow to keep them out of the way. I thought he might continue to take my trousers off, but he left them in place.

"All is well?" Reiter asked.

I licked my lips and nodded. "This is new for me."

"I know," Reiter soothed, running one hand down the flat of my stomach. "May I touch you?"

"Yes," I said, hearing the hitch in my breath.

He smiled next to me, his hands drifting down my lower belly until he wrapped his warm fingers around the base of my shaft and gave it a firm but gentle squeeze. I gasped, my hands jerking a little, but I did not remove them from where my fingers gripped my coat. He stroked his hand up my cock in a movement that made me dizzy for a moment. When he reached the tip, I let out a breathy moan, trying not to squirm too much so he could handle me. He stroked down my shaft again, then up, starting up a slow rhythm that made me whine, my hips jerking when he would reach the tip. "Reiter," I groaned.

"You like that?" he said in a low, slightly smug tone.

"Yes," I whispered. My eyes closed, just letting my body enjoy the sensations of being touched so intimately. I heard rustling, and I opened my eyes to see Reiter still stroking me with one hand while he fumbled with his trouser front with the other. "You can- mm... You can use both hands if you need to."

Reiter's head smirked next to me, and suddenly he enclosed my cock in both of his hands, stroking up and down. I nearly shot up from my prone position, not expecting the new sensation. "Nngh, Reiter!" I gasped, half pleasure, half protest.

Reiter chuckled and let go of me entirely to undo his trousers and pull his own hard cock out. I was not sure what to expect, having never seen another man undressed before me. His own cock was thicker than mine by a not-insubstantial amount, and just as long. I inhaled as I looked at it, my own dick twitching with what I assumed was desire, or maybe jealousy. My fingers clenched tighter above my head, feeling a blush color my face again. "I have never seen another man like this."

Reiter grinned, sliding his hand down to stroke it over his own length. "Would you like to touch it?"

I did want to touch it. I loosed my fingers from above my head and sat up, suddenly much closer to Reiter's chest. I hesitantly reached out and caressed the tip with my palm. It was soft and silky, and I curled my hand curiously around it, giving a slow stroke from top to bottom, the way Reiter had been with me, watching his soft foreskin move under my touch. A shiver ran through him, but he otherwise held still for my ministrations. My fingers traced up the veins on the underside, and he made an appreciative sound when my thumb ran up the underside of the head. I did that again, and he moaned louder, a shudder making him jerk a little toward my touch.

"Am I doing it correctly?" I asked.

Reiter clamped his lips together to hold back what I assumed was a burst of laughter, the sound coming out as a soft snort through his nose. "There is no 'correct' way to do it, Ichabod. I am enjoying it, if that's what you are asking me."

I flushed slightly. As a schoolmaster, doing things 'correctly' had been drilled into me. But I supposed Reiter was right. There were many ways to bring pleasure, and this was entirely new to me. I stroked over his cock again before his hand landed on mine, making me jump and let out a rather inarticulate squeak. Reiter began to tease me with his fingertips. He alternated between that and stroking me with his hand. Shudders were rushing through me, making me moan and gasp and writhe.

Reiter pulled back, and I took the time to catch my breath. "That was amazing."

He laughed long and loud at that. "You have not even spilled yet."

I giggled shyly at that. "I want you to as well."

Reiter rubbed his thumb over my lower lip, and I could taste a bit of saltiness there when my tongue swept over it. "You have so much to explore. And I will explore with you."

I nodded, then nearly leaped out of my skin as Reiter slid further up my hips, and his cock rubbed against mine. My arm flung across my eyes at the unexpected sensation. I peered down between us to watch as Reiter slid his own stiff prick under mine, then closed his large hand around them both, starting to slowly stroke them together. My head tossed to the side in pleasure, and my hands went back up above my head to grip my jacket as I bit my lower lip. His sheath rubbed against the underside of my own, silky and slick. I moaned eagerly as his hand sped up. "Mm. Don't stop," I heard myself say.

"I won't," Reiter said with a chuckle, slowing his hand to give a single long, languid stroke before starting to stroke us both again with renewed energy.

I had only spilled myself a few times in my life. It had never been all that pleasurable, and I was confused why my adolescent male friends would constantly be talking about any sort of passionate encounter, even if it was with their own hand. But now, as Reiter's strong, calloused fingers moved over us, our hips and stiff cocks pressed so firmly to each other, I wondered if perhaps I had simply been waiting for someone to enjoy the experience with. His hand was careful not to stroke too hard but still created such delicious friction between us. His other hand moved to stroke my cheek. I leaned into it, closing my eyes, just letting the heat build between us.

My hips bucked beneath him, though I could not move far with him perched atop me as he was. So I simply lay still and let him rub us together, his hand moving faster and faster. My body burned with delightful heat, drawing sounds out of me that I had never made before. And each one made his head next to me smile. When the ridge on the top of his cock rubbed against the underside of my own where head met shaft, I jerked and tossed my head about. "That," I pleaded desperately, not even sure what I was asking for, but Reiter just chuckled and did it again. I made a sound not unlike the yowling of a cat in heat, thrashing for several enthusiastic strokes before I spilled myself over Reiter's hand, my seed coating my trousers and a bit of his own as well. I collapsed back against the floor, trying to remember how to breathe. Reiter's hand had stilled after I had stopped ejaculating, but I still shuddered with painful pleasure when he carefully pulled his slick hand and cock away from mine.

I moaned, feeling sticky, which was mildly unpleasant, but I did not care enough to move. Until I opened my eyes to see that he still straddled me, cock in hand, unsatisfied. I quickly sat up, so fast that he actually jumped. "May I?" I asked, motioning to his straining shaft.

Reiter moved his hand away in acquiescence, and I wrapped my fingers around him, trying to mimic the way he had held it himself. I began to stroke him back and forth, slowly at first, which I could tell frustrated him with how close he was in his own passion. Once I had figured out a rhythm, I began to move faster, and Reiter let out a groan of pleasure. "Yes," he said through clenched teeth next to me as I worked his cock between my long fingers. Encouraged, I stroked him like that for a few moments before picking up the speed again, watching his foreskin stretch in fascination. And then he let out a yell, his hips jerking, and his seed spilled from the head of his shaft, coating my shirt and hand. I continued to stroke him, as he had me, until he hissed and gently pushed my hand away. "Enough," he chided.

I laughed, wiping the mess on my trouser legs, since they were already messy from my own release. Reiter got off of me and slumped backward, seeming in a daze. Before he could do anything else, I scooped up his head from the floor next to me and planted a kiss firmly on his hot, open mouth. He moaned against my lips. I kissed him for a long moment before pulling him away. I realized with consternation that I had left a sticky smear of seed on his cheek from my hands. "Sorry," I said, starting to swipe at it, but his body leaned over to still my touch before wiping it off himself with his thumb, and then sticking it into his mouth. He moaned, closing his eyes as he seemingly enjoyed the taste of our mingled passions. That sound went down my spine like lightning, despite being slightly mortified at the situation. I had just slaked my carnal lust for the first time with another person, and with someone who, while very much human, was not amongst the living. That felt strange. I wondered for a brief moment if maybe I was going to Hell before I realized that it did not matter. What mattered was Reiter in front of me, his fingers tracing gently over my calf.

Once both of us seemed to have returned to ourselves, I held his head to my chest before moving to cuddle against his warm torso. "Was that all right?" he asked me, and I felt the vibration of his words against my frame.

"Yes," I said. "Did I pleasure you the right way?"

Reiter laughed. "Yes, you were excellent, schoolmaster."

I flushed at that, letting his arms settle around me. I was feeling hot and sticky now, and my clothing definitely needed to be washed, but I did not want to move yet. Something about what we had just done felt important, though I could not articulate exactly what it was. But I wanted it. I wanted to experience it, and more. I wanted to live.

"I am going to help you break this curse," I said suddenly, sitting up from his body and lifting his head to level with mine so quickly that his eyes took a moment to focus.

"What?" he asked.

"I am going to help you break the curse," I said again. "Katrina said that you would be a spirit until the day she died." If there was one thing I had learned about folklore, the way that vows and oaths were worded made all the difference. "If she dies, perhaps your spirit may be set free. And perhaps then the curse would be lifted from Sleepy Hollow."

Reiter seemed surprised by this idea. "I suppose it is possible," he said thoughtfully.

"Have you not tried before?" I asked.

"No," Reiter said. "If I am not on this hallowed ground, I am vulnerable to her. I could be injured or killed like any other mortal." He sighed. "I thought about letting her kill me, many times. But I worried what she might do if the villagers no longer had the Headless Horseman to blame. That she might perhaps curse someone else."

At first, that surprised me, but then I realized how much of a kind-hearted person Reiter really was. It was not in his nature to be violent or to take vengeance. That seemed very much like the sort of thing he would worry about, that someone else would be locked into a lonely existence like his own, and my insides ached once again for his loss.

"If we could lift this curse, together, would you want to?"

Reiter's body straightened in surprise. "I could not ask such a thing of you, Ichabod. You are mortal, and she is very powerful."

"You are not asking me," I said firmly. "I am offering to help."

"No, I could not let you," Reiter replied in a stern tone.

My lips twitched in a smile. "Perhaps then it is good that I have never been one for doing as I am told."

Reiter sighed heavily. "Ichabod..."

"What are my other choices?" I demanded. "I flee, only to be stuck here in these woods until the villagers find me and burn me. I die on Halloween, and you continue to exist in this half-life of sacrifices, watching Sleepy Hollow be trapped in time. Why should I not attempt to free you and the other villagers from her? I have nothing left to lose."

"But I could lose you," Reiter pointed out.

"I am going to die if we do nothing," I responded, the words bitter on my tongue. "If we can break the spell holding you here, even if I die, at least you will not have to live through more lifetimes of sacrifices."

"Killing a witch, let alone two witches and a minion, is no easy task," Reiter said. "And you are too good to let that darkness consume you."

"Perhaps I was," I said. "But I have you now, and you have me. And I do not want you to suffer."

Reiter was silent for a moment before he nodded against my chest. "All right. We will try."

"That is all I ask," I replied, leaning back into his comforting embrace.

Chapter Eight

If Katrina was coming after me, she was not making much of an effort. I supposed that knowing that the curse would end me whether she wasted time hunting me or not made her unconcerned about my movements. However, it seemed that her powers over Sleepy Hollow were not as strong without having my full soul to draw upon. The winter was unusually harsh that year, and multiple animals had died. I could hear grumbles of it from the townspeople. The blame was entirely directed at me for not dying on Halloween. My body still had not been found, so they did not know if I was alive or dead, but most assumed I had been chased to some deep part of the woods that they dared not venture to, and my grave was there amongst the shadows.

"The townspeople are used to the glen being a strange gathering place for all manner of spirits and spooks," Reiter had told me. "The land itself is uneasy and wild. There are voices upon the air, and all manner of otherworldly sightings." He made sure that he was one of those sightings, being glimpsed once in a while through the trees on one of his rides, or as he slipped away from the village. No one ever came after him if they did see him. I believe the fear of the Headless Horseman was strong enough that none dared to risk his wrath.

Every few days, my heart would surge in agony that would drop me into darkness, and smaller reverberations would make me double over to catch my breath. I had no mirror, save for the windows of the church, but I could tell that the stripping of my soul was taking a toll on me. My strength would ebb and flow, and I could see a ghoulish gauntness in my eyes and cheeks when I caught a glimpse of my own reflection. I tried not to think too hard about what that might mean as the months marched on.

I had the winter and spring to plan. I was going to search the Van Tassel house, every building, every nook and cranny, until I found Reiter's skull. But I had to sneak around the property when I knew Katrina and Brom would not be there. The summer months would afford me plenty of opportunities. The nice weather and longer hours of sun meant that the villagers were often out late, shops were open, dinner parties were had. I became adept at sneaking through the woods to listen to the townspeople talk and had a pretty good idea when Katrina would be away from the manor. Baltus rarely left the Van Tassel property, but his movements were quite predictable. He was a man of schedule, so his routes walking the grounds, talking to the various servants, and doing his paperwork were easy to determine.

I decided to search the outer buildings first, before trying to slip inside the house where there were always servants bustling around. That made me think that perhaps Katrina would have hidden the skull outside of the house as well so that no one stumbled upon it while cleaning. Once summer came, and there was no mud or snow to reveal my footprints, I began my search of the Van Tassel property.

I would search later in the afternoon so I had a few good hours of light to see by before I would sneak back to the woods after sundown, where Reiter would meet me on the back of Daredevil. He was silent as a shadow, and more than once I had the life nearly scared out of me by him materializing nearby. Then we'd swiftly ride back to the hallowed grounds and cross the bridge so we were safe from the villagers or any witches that might be on the lookout for us. I knew Reiter did not like me outside the safety of the church, but I felt I could not simply sit on my hands and wait for my inevitable end. I had to at least attempt to help him and the rest of the townsfolk, even if my very soul was at risk every time I left the eastern area.

My search of the first few barns on the Van Tassel property were unsuccessful beyond scaring a coop full of chickens and nearly being kicked in the head by one of the horses. But during my second visit, while I crouched in the hay loft as two of the lads from the town came in to do some work, I overheard a conversation that lifted my spirits.

"I think there's something going on with Miss Katrina," the one I knew as Philip said. "She ain't lookin' as bright as she usually is."

"The winter was hard on all of us, but she's looking a little rough earlier than usual," agreed Pieter.

"She gets so drawn after the harvest," Philip said. "But after the party, she perks right up again."

"Every part of her," Pieter chuckled, and they slapped each other jovially upon the shoulder.

When I brought up this conversation to Reiter, he seemed thoughtful, as if searching his memories. "I know that ensuring a bountiful harvest takes a lot of her strength, both magically and physically," he said. "I assume this past winter was harder than usual on the town because she did not have your full soul to draw from. I wonder if, by the time of the harvest party, she has used up most of her magic?"

I recalled how Katrina had looked a little sickly at the last harvest party, even though she was still a beauty. Presumably she had had the previous victim's full soul at her disposal and yet still had seemed quite drained. "That is certainly as good a guess as any," I said. My own knowledge of magic and witchcraft was limited, but I would imagine that cursing someone's soul would take quite a bit of magic. "If she is not at her peak on Halloween, might that be the best time to strike?"

"She will have the entire village assembled," Reiter said doubtfully.

"You told me that if there are no outsiders, one of the villagers is chosen," I said. "If they knew the truth, that Katrina was selecting from amongst them to die, might they turn on her?"

"It is possible," Reiter said, though I could hear the uncertainty in his voice. "That would be quite the gamble."

"This entire thing is a gamble," I pointed out. "One that we will lose if we do nothing."

Reiter sighed and held me close. "You are right about that." So it was decided. We would wait until Halloween and the harvest party, in the hopes that Katrina's power would be depleted, giving us our best chance to strike her a fatal blow.

My third visit to the Van Tassel property left me with two more outbuildings to search. The first yielded nothing of value. The second was their root cellar, and I had nearly despaired of finding what I was looking for when, toward the back, I found a single wooden trap door, covered by a large pile of baskets. I moved them cautiously, heart in my ears as I reached down to pull at the creaking wood. I was glad for my thin frame as I slipped down into the darkness, finding a ladder there that went downward a few steps.

I had a lantern with me, and I lit it now with a shaking hand. I half-expected to find Katrina flying out of the shadows at me, or some dreadful manner of spook or goblin, but the musty hole held no living horrors, save for a few spiders who scuttled away from my light.

I swiveled around in the small space. It was not much larger than a priest's confessional, with nothing inside it at all, until my eyes landed on a wooden door, hidden in shadow, at the back. I crept forward, checking the handle, expecting to find it locked. Instead, it gave under my touch, and the door swung silently inward. I lifted my lantern high to throw its feeble light as far as I could, and then nearly dropped it as I clapped my hand to my mouth and nose to contain a scream of fright.

I nearly made a dash out of there, but this was what I had come for. I steeled my nerves and entered the low-ceilinged room. It was made from earth like the root cellar, but crevices had been carved into the wall like shelves. And inset into these shelves were skulls. Dozens of them, the light of my lantern flickering over their empty eyes and glinting teeth.

I looked around the room in despair. There were dozens, possibly even a hundred or more, skulls of various sizes and degradation. A few I could see were children, their adult teeth still imbedded inside of their oral cavities. I drew in a shuddering breath, clapping my hand to my mouth to keep from making any other noise. Every which way I turned, my frail lantern beam caught more and more rows of grinning mouths, empty sockets, and shining foreheads. I felt as if I had stepped into a crypt, and all of the skulls would perhaps turn to gape at me and begin to whisper my name in hideous tones.

How could I possibly tell which one was Reiter's skull? I could eliminate the children and a few of the smaller skulls that looked like they might be female or more petite men, but beyond that, there was little to distinguish them. A few were missing teeth here or there, or had what looked like healed injuries in a few places. I knew that Reiter had very nice teeth overall except for the top right front tooth that was twisted at an angle. That was what I looked for as I studied each one in turn, trying to envision whose face might have covered each of these canvases of bone.

I wondered if the skulls were placed on the shelves in any particular order and started to work my way around, trying to find the berth that held the oldest-looking ones. It was not a great plan, but it was the only one I had at the moment. I was looking at two skulls of similar nature, twisting my lantern this way and that to see if I could find anything that might distinguish them, when a flash of something bright caught the corner of my eye. I held up my lantern to look. It took me a moment before I found the source, because it was on the ground rather than on a shelf.

A solitary pumpkin, of good size, was tucked into a corner next to the wall. The pumpkin looked as fresh as the day it had been picked, though it was late summer now, well beyond when pumpkins would have survived the winter, and much too soon before they would be ready this season. I had learned from the farmers in Sleepy Hollow that pumpkins would not be ready to harvest until early October, but this one looked to be as perfect as any I had ever seen. I knelt next to it, examining it with my lantern light. At the very top, around the stem, was a thin line, as if made by a large cutting knife. My heart gave a leap in my chest as I reached for the stem and carefully lifted it off. It was quite heavy, and I set it aside and peered in.

The inside was hollow, though the pumpkin smell was fresh as though it had only been carved out. And nestled inside of it, as if it was natural for pumpkins to grow their own, was a skull. An old one, larger than a child. And when I shifted it carefully to examine it, I could see that its front right tooth was twisted slightly in the same way that Reiter's revealed when he smiled. This had to be his skull. I could almost see the outline of the kind face of the man I knew upon it, with dark hair, mahogany eyes, and thin lips.

My heart gave another joyful leap, and then I quickly picked up the pumpkin lid and replaced it. My fingers itched to take it now, to carry it straight back to Reiter and reunite him with that which was once his, but I could not betray my presence here. Once the pumpkin appeared to be whole again, I rose and swiftly made my way out of the room, closing the door once more to the chamber of horrors. I clambered back up the ladder into the main root cellar, where I still seemed to be unobserved. I replaced the wooden trap door and then moved the baskets back into position on top of it until I was satisfied my visit would be unnoticed. I peeked out of the cellar to find the sun starting to set and cast long shadows over the world, stretching the Van Tassel manor toward the woods, as if it were reaching, searching out the Horseman. Ducking low, I made my way into the cover of trees to my appointed meeting spot with Reiter.

When we had returned to the hallowed ground once more, I told him about the room with all of the skulls and how to access it. His dark eyes almost danced in delight before he became very stern. "I do not want you to leave the safety of the churchyard again until we go after her."

I nodded in agreement. My task had been completed, I knew where to find Reiter's skull. "I promise I will not," I said, lifting his head up to seal the promise with a kiss upon his lips. He folded me into his arms from behind as I held his head close to mine.

In the months following our first intimacy together, we had done the same a few times, though only when I would initiate a time of kissing and petting. I had not yet been fully bare in front of him, and Reiter always wore his shirt and waistcoat with its black covering over the stump of his neck. I never pushed him to reveal more than he wanted to, and he was respectful of all of my limits and concerns, even if it meant one or neither of us did not satisfy ourselves when we came to further passions. Just the touch of his hands on me was enough, to press close in the darkness and know he was there.

Tonight, his kiss met mine with a strange, new ferocity that I tried to meet in my own awkward way. I grasped his cheeks to kiss him firmly as his body pressed behind me, and I could already feel his cock straining in his trousers against my back. "Are you so eager?" I asked with a small grin at him.

He looked a little sheepish. "You do not even know the things that you do to me, Ichabod."

That brought a blush to my gaunt cheeks. "You have showed me."

"I have showed you some," he agreed, and his hands slid eagerly down my front to grasp me through my breeches while suddenly grinding up against me from behind. "I want to show you more. I want to worship your body and watch you come undone. Hearing your pleasure is my greatest delight."

I was sure I was as pink as a virgin milkmaid at the words, ducking my head a little. "Is it?" I asked breathily before our lips met again in a searing kiss, my fingers tangling in his long, dark hair.

When we finally pulled away again, my heart racing under my ribs, his body ground against my back once more. "Would you like to learn more of the ways I can pleasure you?" he purred. His voice held an invitation, a plea, that made my skin heat and my blood tingle in my veins.

I swallowed hard, feeling his back plaster to me, and despite the layers of fabric between us, I could feel the desire radiating from him such as I had never felt from him before. A shiver went through me to the marrow of my bones. Until meeting Reiter, I had never experienced lust for anyone. I had even wondered for a time if I was not meant to, for while I could appreciate a pleasing form of either a man or a woman, I had never felt the desire to sate myself between spread legs or an open mouth. But here, with Reiter's warmth behind me, the weight of his head heavy in my hands, I wanted it. I felt wanton desire flare inside of me, a yearning beginning to throb between my legs. "Show me." My voice was no more than a whisper, but it was all the permission he needed.

Reiter's hands slid down my front, fingers working deftly at the buttons of my waistcoat, and then my shirt. His fingers splayed over my chest, stroking with his fingertips, and I marveled that a spirit that could ride through the forest the way he did could be so gentle. He slid my shirt off my shoulders, baring my chest to the air that suddenly seemed much warmer than it had been. I flushed with the urge to wrap my arms around myself, but I was distracted by the sudden brush of his lips against my palm where both rested in my lap. That made me jump, and he made an appreciative sound as he kissed over the heel of my hand, and then over the pads of my fingers. He drew one of my fingers into his mouth and began to suck lightly on it. I moaned, my other hand brushing a few strands of his dark hair away from his jaw, watching the way his lips and cheeks moved over my finger, his tongue teasing and tickling.

Behind me, Reiter's hands traced over my back, fingertips brushing the outline of each of my ribs, making me writhe. His fingers lit me up like a bonfire on my skin. Just that touch alone was so incredible, I felt like a might forget how to breathe. One hand slid around in front to grasp one of my nipples, rolling it firmly between his finger and thumb, while the other snaked down to undo my trousers. I leaned back against him, my hand that was not occupied by his tongue sliding up to wrap around his bicep and hold him tightly. His arms were so strong beneath his clothing.

He fished my cock out of my trousers and stroked it languidly several times, making me shudder in pleasure. He moaned a laugh around my finger. "Easy, little virgin. I want to explore you."

"Yes," I whispered. He shifted me around so he could pull off my stockings and trousers, each one falling away like a shed skin, until I leaned back against his chest and realized that I was now completely naked. For the first time in my adult life, I was utterly bare in front of someone other than myself. I flushed and started to pull my legs up, but Reiter's strong hands slid down my bare hips to push my knees apart.

"I want to see you," he said. His head still rested on the floor in front of me, and I felt a moment of panic as I realized that spreading my legs now would expose everything to him at a most intimate level.

"You do not have to be ashamed," he said soothingly, one of his hands running down my chest and back up, like stroking the belly of an agitated dog. "It is just me."

I licked my lips, then nodded, shifting back against his torso for more support before I slowly spread my legs and sank down just a bit. His head rested just past my spread knees. His hands slid down my ribs, then up to tweak one of my nipples, making me jump. My cock was standing at full attention now, and I clenched my fingers into the legs of his trousers to keep from trying to cover myself. I saw his eyes drift over me, the length of my cock, over my balls, and even lower. I started to squirm, until his hand slid down and began to stroke me. I gasped, my legs instinctively spreading wider for his touch, and he grinned. "Yes, sweet one. Let me see all of you." His hand moved on me, pausing at the crown of my shaft to brush his thumb up the underside, and I tensed, moaning at the pleasure. "Mm. You look so tight, my little virgin."

I blushed red from head to toe, and he chuckled. "Do you want to experience me inside of you?"

I swallowed hard, fingers giving a slight yank at his trousers where I held them. "I... What part of you?"

Reiter laughed, so much that his body that still held me also shook with laughter. I wasn't sure whether to laugh with him or to feel utterly embarrassed at my naïveté. But he slid his free hand up to grip my chin lightly from behind. "Why don't we start with fingers and see how you feel?"

His words made my face burn, but my cock gave an eager little twitch. "Yes," I said.

"Then on your knees, sweet one," he purred as his hands gently lifted me away from him, and he rose to his feet.

"Where are you going?" I asked.

"Just getting something to prepare you," Reiter said. "If you are on your hands and knees, I can talk to you while I do it."

I hesitantly shifted so I was on all fours, feeling slightly mortified at how exposed I was, and more than a little glad that this church was not disturbed. "Like this?"

"Mm, lower your arms a little," he said. I bent my elbows to bring my face closer to the floor. His head leaned in and stole a firm kiss from my mouth. "Perfect."

I sputtered with laughter at that, jerking upward again. "You are a tease!"

"Oh no," Reiter said with a smug smile. "It is you who tease me, Ichabod, with every movement you make."

I blushed at that, then heard the creak of wood as the Horseman's body returned. He had taken off his jacket, leaving him in his black shirtsleeves and waistcoat, the black cover still over the stump of his neck as well. He folded his jacket, then suddenly grasped me around the waist, lifting me easily with his supernatural strength. I squeaked, and he tucked the folded jacket under my knees before settling me back in place. I flushed. "You do not have to do that."

"I know," he said. "Now, look at me."

I turned away from his body to face his head again, and he leaned in to give me a soft kiss. "If you want to stop, we can. I only want to make you feel good."

I smiled. "I know you do."

I heard the stopper come out of a bottle, and I instinctively turned to look. "What is that?"

"Oil," Reiter said, holding it up for me to see.

I blushed at the realization that it would likely be some of the church's oil, perhaps for anointing. Well, I had already done quite a bit of desecration of this holy space, no reason to balk at it now. The edge of the bottle touched my lower back, and then something wet dribbled down into my most intimate place. I shivered, my fingers clenching into fists at the unusual sensation. Then I felt one of Reiter's fingers gently circle my hole. I swallowed hard, turning my eyes to meet Reiter's again. "You have done this before?"

"Yes," he said soothingly, and I felt some of my tension release as his other hand kneaded the flesh of my spread buttocks, his finger dipping and teasing but not pushing into me yet.

"Have you ever, mm, been on this end of it?" I asked. Why I felt the need to make conversation while he was doing this, I did not know, but it seemed to be calming my apprehension.

"I have done it to myself before," Reiter said thoughtfully. "But not with someone else. When I am with someone, I like this." He gave one of my cheeks a firm squeeze, and I squeaked again. His head gave me a soft kiss on the cheek. "May I enter you?"

My hole clenched at that before I willed myself to relax. "Yes," I said breathily.

His finger massaged me a moment more, and I tried not to tense, until his fingertip breeched my sphincter, just the first inch. I gasped, clenching a little, which sent a spark of strange pleasure through my belly. He drew his finger back and out of me, and I moaned softly. His finger entered again, then pulled back, not all the way out this time, starting up a gentle rhythm where he sank deeper each time his finger pushed forward. I could feel it burning, the deeper he went, before it was soothed again by sweet friction as his finger withdrew and then returned again. "So tight," he moaned, and I felt slightly delighted I was able to watch his face in front of me as his finger moved. His eyes were half-closed, his lips slightly parted as his finger pulled back and pushed in again. I moaned, my hips suddenly pressing back toward him of their own accord. He grinned, his dark eyes opening to look at me fully. "You like that?"

"Yes," I groaned, my hips giving a little wiggle, and he twisted his finger inside of me, adding a new sensation that flooded my brain with pleasure.

"Can I add another?" he asked, and I gave a hazy nod. When he drew back to enter me again, this time a second oiled finger pushed at my virgin hole, and I whimpered. "Only for a moment," he soothed. The second finger popped inside of me, stretching my hole wider, and I gasped, pressing my cheek against the floor. It sank deeper into me until the two fingers were seated together inside of me. "Good," he soothed, his other hand stroking down my back lightly, which made me arch, tightening my hole in turn.

He worked his fingers inside of me for a minute as I moaned and shivered. Then he drew his fingers back before sliding them inside me again, then back, starting up a slow rhythm. My breath caught as my hips started to move with his thrusts, pushing back to plunge his digits deeper inside of me. The pain was lessening now, my body relaxing around his wonderful fingers as I rocked my hips back and forth.

Reiter let out a breath. “I wish you could see yourself right now. You look so beautiful, riding my fingers like that. You have me spellbound.”

I flushed with pleasure, loving the words of praise as his fingers moved in and out. “Ready for more?” he asked, and I nodded eagerly. The next moment, there were three fingers buried inside me. I let out a cry, my hips stilling for a moment as my body protested the intrusion. I felt something wet slide inside of me and realized he had poured more oil over the area before beginning to move his fingers again. I moaned, pressing my cheek into the cool wood planks beneath me. I had been so focused on his fingers that I had hardly noticed that my cock was dripping between my legs until a sticky bead landed on my inner thigh. “So tight,” he purred again, his fingers twisting inside of me and drawing a cry of pleasure from my lips. “I bet I could make you spill your seed just with my fingers, sweet virgin.”

I opened my eyes to look at him from where my face was pressed to the wood. “Yes,” I pleaded.

“No,” he said, his eyes narrowing sweetly. “It is your first time, and I want it to be the most memorable pleasure of your life.”

His words went straight to my balls, which tightened eagerly in response to his words. He laughed and gave them a brush with one fingertip. “So eager. Do you want to feel my cock inside of your tight, virgin hole?”

“Yes,” I moaned. “Please, Reiter.”

His hand stilled for a moment at that, and I opened my eyes, glancing back at him before turning to his head again, afraid I had said something wrong, but he just smiled. “I like it when you use my name.”

“If... if I can talk,” I groaned. He laughed, and then his fingers slid out of me, one by one. I moaned at the loss, my hole clenching and aching as cool air touched me. I heard the fumble of trouser laces, and my cock gave an eager little jump against my stomach.

“Are you ready for me?” Reiter asked, and I heard his slick hand stroking over his shaft.

“Please,” I moaned, leaning in to give him a firm kiss, holding his head with my fingers so I did not kiss him too hard and knock him over.

He moaned against my mouth and dipped his tongue over my lips, then past my teeth, just as his body slid up behind me, and I felt something much larger than a finger press to my entrance. I whimpered but focused on kissing him. Reiter obliged, kissing me back with equal passion as his strong hands grabbed my hips and began to push forward into my hole. I whined against his mouth, letting him do the moving, guiding my hips back as he pushed into me, so deep I thought I might not be able to breathe. When his hips were flush against my spread cheeks, he broke our kiss to murmur, “So good, sweet one. You’re doing so good.”

“Doing so well,” I couldn’t stop myself from saying breathlessly.

Reiter stared at me, then cocked a brow. “If you are still able to correct me, I am not pleasuring you enough.”

I blushed absolutely crimson. “I’m sorry.”

Reiter laughed, and then drew back his hips and began to rock in and out of me at a slow, steady pace. I cried out, arching a little as his great heat thrust inside of me, stretching me wide. My cock bobbed with each movement of his hips. I could feel my passion building low in my belly. And then Reiter's hips pushed into me and went still. I clenched around his length, glancing back at him in surprise. He suddenly leaned over to pull me off my hands so I was only on my knees, the change of angle making my toes curl and my hole tighten. "I am going to please you in a way that no other man can," Reiter purred, and a shiver went through me.

"You already have," I whispered back.

He hummed a soft laugh before his hands slid down my hips and went around me. I braced my own hands on his thighs, unsure what he was doing, until he lifted his head from in front of me, and then the wet warmth of his mouth closed over the tip of my cock. I let out a sound I was sure I had never made before in my life, my fingers clenching in the fabric of his trousers. My passage tightened around him, and he let out a soft sound of appreciation as he guided his own head down my length, inch by inch, each one sweet agony as I writhed under the movement.

If I had thought I was feeling pleasure before, I was eating my words now. My mouth was open wide, cries and moans and tiny screams escaping my throat. My hands reached behind us to clutch desperately at his hips, unsure where else to put them. And then he began to move again, his hips thrusting in and out of me, his hands moving his head in rhythm so when he thrust his dick deep inside me, it also pushed my hips forward into his eager mouth, his tongue rubbing the underside of my cock. He made soft noises as he swallowed around me with each thrust, and I had momentary illogical concern that he would not be able to breathe before the shove of his hips deep inside of me made me see stars and unable to form any more coherent thoughts.

Each thrust of his cock inside of me drove a cry of pleasure from my lips, trying to form words that I was sure were nothing more than babbling sounds, my voice raised in praise the likes of which that church had never seen. I yanked at his trouser legs, so violently I might have ripped them in two without knowing it. When my passion spilled out of me only moments later, my vision went white, and I lost all ability to do anything but scream as my cock bucked inside Reiter's mouth.

Still the stimulation continued as he thrust into me, his tongue and throat working eagerly over me as my over-sensitized cock jumped, a whine of pleasurable torment escaping my throat, his arm around my waist and cock inside of me the only things holding me upright. If the pain from Katrina taking my soul from my body was unbearable agony, this delicious torture was the answer to it. He grunted around my length, making my cock give another feeble pulse in his mouth before he thrust once more, deep inside of me and stayed there, gripping my hips as his own pleasure rocked through him, sending a shudder through his entire form against my back.

I do not know how long we stayed there, him plastered against my back as I gripped him. I only know that when he pulled out of me, my body felt a cold, hollow loss, and then I was lying on the floor, curled on my side as I breathed. His head rested next to me, his forehead against the top of my hair, and he pulled his jacket from under my knees to drape it over me. I drifted in a haze for a very long time, content to just have him near me as my eyes closed into the best sleep I had had in a very long time.

When I woke up, Reiter had already cleaned himself up, put aside my clothes, and had heated water for me to wash. “You are such a gentleman,” I teased as I cleansed myself with the water and cloth.

He sat and watched me from the front pew, head once again resting on his lap. “Should I not be?”

I laughed at that. “I appreciate that you are.” I had pulled on my pants and was reaching for my shirtsleeves when the sudden burst of agony hit me. I screamed, my hands clasping to my chest. Water spilled, and I heard Reiter saying my name over and over as I spiraled once more into darkness.

When I awoke later from the wave of pain, Reiter and I were curled on a bed of blankets on the dais again, his front pressed to my back as he stroked my hair gently. The warm weight of his head was against my chest, and I could see that his head was tipped so he could listen to my heartbeat as he rested there against me. I nestled back into his embrace.

"Has it all passed?" he asked.

"Yes," I assured him, relaxing back against him. "Thank you for taking care of me."

"Always," he said. "I am so sorry you are having to endure this torment."

I threaded my fingers with his. "I would rather experience this torment with you by my side than never having met you."

He let out a soft sigh. "I have never known true peace until you were here with me."

My heart ached at that as I stroked his hair, his temple resting against my torso as he cuddled me from behind. "I always want you to feel that way."

"Ichabod," he said softly, and I shifted so we could better see eye-to-eye. "If we succeed, and I no longer exist in this world, will you be all right?"

The question gave me pause. Reiter had lived alone for so long. If this plan failed, I would die, and he would once again be alone, trapped between worlds, watching people be killed in his name. But if we succeeded, there was no telling what would happen to him. Perhaps his soul would leave forever, hopefully to find peace, but where would that leave me? In the same position I had been in before I met him, but bereft of the only person in my life who had ever mattered to me, the only person I could say truly loved me. I would have to go on without him. "I would hurt," I said honestly. "For a very long time. But if it brings you peace after all you have suffered, that will be a comfort to me."

He was silent for a long moment before his arms tightened around me just a little more. "If I am no longer with you, I wish every happiness upon you. I wish for you to find love, a greater love than I, and to never feel sorrow a day in your life."

Tears made their way silently down my cheeks as I squeezed his hands. "I will always love you," I said, taking his palm and pressing it to my chest where my heart beat inside of it. "As long as I live, until I die, whether that is tomorrow or a hundred years, I will always love you."

His hand pressed to my chest, as ferociously as if he wished to keep my heart trapped inside of me. I would have given everything in the world for us to stay right there and never move again, for time to stop and for us to simply be.

Chapter Nine

The harvest was not as plentiful as it usually was; the storehouses would barely make it through the winter. Reiter heard whispers of it amongst the townspeople almost constantly. I hoped that this would work in our favor. He had glimpsed Katrina a few times and said that she indeed looked more haggard than she usually did. It gave me pleasure to think that she was struggling, having only patchwork pieces of my soul to work with.

The evening of the harvest party, neither of us talked as we sat side by side on the church steps, watching the sun sink behind the trees. His hand clutched my own, his head resting on my lap. Late in the afternoon, we would catch occasional sounds of the villagers making their way toward the Van Tassel estate. Wagon wheels scraping along, horses clip-clopping, a joyful burst of laughter. It was so strange to me to think that in only a few hours, one of those cheerful people would fall victim to the dark witch and her blood magic, and whatever poor soul it was would have no idea until it was too late. If I could put a stop to it, I had to do it. Not only for my own sake, or even for Reiter, but for the sake of every person in the village who unknowingly suffered under the Van Tassel family's cruelty.

As the last rays of the sun vanished behind the tree trunks, the soft sound of hooves crunched the nearby leaves of the churchyard, and the shadowy, black steed appeared from around the side of the church. Reiter smiled and scooped his head from my lap before his body rose and moved over to take the reins that were already attached to the horse's head. He stroked over its side, and I heard him crooning to it, pressing his forehead to the horse's. Daredevil rumbled and nudged him back, and I smiled at that. If Reiter was able to pass on to the afterlife, I hoped the majestic steed would go with him so they could ride together.

Reiter came back to me, pulling on his riding gloves before offering his hand to me. I took it and let him help me up from the churchyard steps. "Ready?" he asked.

"Yes," I said, determined to not let my courage fail me in this final hour.

Reiter set his head on the pommel of the saddle, then lifted me up with both hands on my hips so I could sit behind the saddle on the massive beast, who flicked his tail and whickered. Reiter stepped into the stirrup and slung himself over the back of Daredevil with practiced ease. I wrapped my arms around his strong waist, and then we were trotting through the churchyard, past the final resting places of early Sleepy Hollow residents, onto the path, toward the bridge. I glanced back at the church that had been my home for almost a year, and Reiter's haven for many more. I wondered if he was sad to leave it, or perhaps scared that he would come back to it alone in only a few hours' time.

We reached the bridge, and the hollow clop of hooves on it echoed around us as the cold stream rushed below. Just before we reached the end of the bridge, Reiter pulled Daredevil to a stop, his hand sliding to catch mine around his waist. "I love you."

"I love you too," I said, giving his hand a squeeze back. And then he nudged the steed over the final steps onto the path.

Nothing came for us. No monster swooped down from the sky or burst from the bushes. The wind did not even change. It was just us and Daredevil, trotting through the woods, as peaceful as if we were out for a romantic evening ride. Reiter turned the horse into the trees, and we followed the stream north through the foliage until we reached the border of Sleepy Hollow. We then turned west, toward the Hudson and the Van Tassel estate, silent as shadows amongst the trees. I could feel my strength waning the closer we got to the house, and I imagined I looked quite the sight, with sunken eyes and cheeks. I probably looked more corpse-like than Reiter himself. Hopefully my awful appearance would spook the townsfolk even more upon my arrival.

We had laid out our plan in advance, though we knew it nearly all depended on chance and luck. Reiter would go to the room below the root cellar to grab his skull, which, we hoped, would give him the power to strike at Katrina. Meanwhile, I would enter the party, with all of the village present, and tell them what the Van Tassels had been doing to them. With luck on our side, the townsfolk would be outraged and turn on Katrina and Baltus, and Reiter could strike them both down, perhaps in full view of the town so they would realize he was not their enemy.

It was not an elaborate plan, nor even a great one. If it all was to succeed, we would need a miracle from Heaven above for us both to come out unscathed. I was sure that at least one of us would not live to see the dawn. That made my heart grow even heavier in my chest as we drew near to the Van Tassel farm, where light glowed from every window, and laughter and music hid the evil that lurked within.

We halted at the edge of the trees, and Reiter jumped down before helping me off of Daredevil. He lifted his head from the pommel and held it out to me so I could take it in my hands. The kiss we shared tasted of salt tears.

"Be strong, sweet one," Reiter said, cupping my cheek in his gloved hand.

"I will, my Horseman," I said, wrapping one arm around him while holding his head with the other. I did not want to let go, to have him whisked away from me forever. I wanted to stand there in the moonlight for all eternity, under the creaking trees of Sleepy Hollow.

"I will come for you," he promised, his voice low and even more ragged than usual.

"I know," I said, pressing my forehead to his. "I love you, Reiter."

"I love you, Ichabod Crane," he said. We shared a last kiss before I surrendered Reiter's head back to him. He swung up onto Daredevil's back and snapped the reins, and then he and his ink-black steed melted like shadows into the trees once more.

The back door of the house to the kitchen was open so the servants could easily go to the well and probably to let the cool evening breeze into the stifling room. I crossed the flat land from the forest to the doorway quickly, feeling Reiter's eyes on me the entire time. I reached the door, took a deep breath, and then stepped inside the kitchen as if I owned it.

It took a moment for someone to notice me in the busy space, but one of the maids looked up from where she was wiping clean some of the silver utensils. She screamed, and the forks fell to the floor with a clatter. The next moment, everyone in the kitchen turned to look at me. A few shouted, one fainted, a few made hasty warding gestures, as if I was a spirit from the grave. I ignored them all, striding through the kitchen and into the large living area where the majority of the guests were gathered.

The band was playing, some of the villagers dancing by the firelight as others stood around and talked. It looked as festive as it had last year, though now I could see it for the death celebration that it was. Those closest to where I entered stopped their conversations. Someone screamed, and within seconds, the entire room had gone silent, every set of eyes trained on me.

I knew the importance of not running. If I left the safety of the eyes of the townsfolk, Katrina and Brom could transform into their beastly creatures and easily take me down. As long as the villagers were there, Katrina would hopefully not be able to use magic against me. Visibly, at least, I reminded myself. Of course, we were dealing with an unknown force, and I was taking a massive gamble.

My skin crawled and itched with the weight of dozens of gazes, but I forced myself to pretend I was entirely alone, crossing over to the table and picking up one of the sweet cakes there, taking a bite, as if my presence were entirely welcome. I glanced around and spotted Katrina across the room, standing with a group of young women and children. Brom was by the fireplace, a cup of ale in his hand, and Baltus was sitting in a chair in the corner, a pipe forgotten in his hand and curling long whisps of smoke into the air.

Madam Von Brussett stepped forward. "Master Crane!" she gasped, and she sounded less than pleased to see me. "We thought the Horseman had killed you!"

"Oh no, I am very much alive, thank you!" I said, giving a gracious bow toward her.

I watched Katrina and Brom exchange glances across the room at each other, and I knew what was about to come, steeling myself to hold my ground and speak before either of them could. "I do have quite the tale to tell. Of curses, and horsemen, and witches," I said, saying the last word directly to Katrina, whose smile didn't falter for an instant. The firelight flickered over her hollow eyes and gaunt cheeks, making her appear more wraith-like than human.

Brom suddenly stepped forward, giving me a harsh glare. "We'll have none of your fairy stories here, Ichabod Crane! The Horseman was supposed to take you for his blood sacrifice so the town would thrive. Because of you, Sleepy Hollow is struggling."

I glowered back at him. "The Horseman is not the one who controls the prosperity of the town," I said, making sure my voice was loud enough for everyone to hear, as if addressing a room full of misbehaving children. "He is simply the scapegoat for the one who does." I turned to look at her. "The dark witch, Katrina Van Tassel."

A muffled murmur ran through the crowd, and I felt my breath catch in my throat. Katrina just gazed back at me. "That is quite the accusation against my daughter, Master Crane," said Baltus suddenly from the corner, rising from his chair. "What proof do you have that Katrina is a witch?"

All eyes were on me again, and I felt like I had swallowed a sharp bone that had lodged itself in my throat. "The Horseman told me," I replied firmly. "I have seen her magic for myself."

"Oh, have you?" Baltus said, stepping forward a few paces. He spread his arms wide to encompass the room. "I see no Horseman here now. I see only a troubled, young outsider, standing amidst us, accusing my daughter of a most heinous crime. Give us some evidence, good sir, or be exposed for the consummate liar that you are."

"Do you not think it strange, that no one in this town has ever died, except by the Horseman's hand?" I asked. "That the years pass, but Annabelle never grows in her adult teeth, or that Dirk never gets any taller? That your skin does not wrinkle, your bodies do not age, you do not fall ill? That no new babies are born? Everything remains the same, including you."

A few glances were exchanged amongst the partygoers before Ezra Brouwer suddenly turned to me. "Let's say ye be tellin' the truth, Master Crane. Why should that concern us? We live here, we're safe and healthy, we never die. Isn't that what anyone should want?"

My guts clenched inside of me at the murmured assent that seemed to go around the room. "She is killing people to do it," I protested.

"Outsiders," someone commented.

"But when there are no outsiders, she has killed your family, your friends, your children! Someone must die each year." I looked around desperately at the villagers. "You all are under the thumb of the Van Tassels. They do not care about you. You are but sheep for slaughter!"

"The Horseman killed them," Brom said firmly. "He chooses who lives and who dies."

"Katrina chooses," I shot back. "She is the one who curses the victims and kills them. Cursed me. She and Brom chased me through the woods last Halloween to try to murder me. The Horseman saved me."

Katrina laughed, and all eyes suddenly turned to her. "You are cursed, Master Crane? You are the reason this past year has been so hard? How ungracious, after all we have done for you. But there is still time to make amends." Her blue eyes flashed as she pointed one long finger at me. "Capture him. We will burn him, and rid Sleepy Hollow of the pestilence he has wrought upon us!"

My body went icy cold. I was suddenly aware of being surrounded on all sides; even the servants were now blocking the door to the kitchen behind me. I still thought that to be my best option, so I turned and made a mad dash for the kitchen doorway. I was hopelessly too slow. The crowd surged, and my arms were grabbed. My jacket was torn from me in the scuffle, and several blows landed upon my face and my torso, forcing the air from me. I spun, catching myself against the mantle with my forehead. A skull grinned back at me from the decorations there, this one older than the one I remembered from last year, with a slightly twisted front tooth. And then hands were upon me in my dazed state, dragging me away, my heart pounding in my ears, blood trickling from the cut above my eyebrow.

The villagers hauled me outside into the night, the cool air and darkness a sudden shock to my system after the warmth and brightness of the house. Orders were shouted about, but I could hear almost none of it over the sound of my own heartbeat and the blood surging in my ears. I tried to struggle, but my limbs were held fast. I vaguely wondered what time it was. It still had to be several hours until midnight, I thought.

My hands and legs were threaded through a ladder that someone had grabbed, tying them painfully in place so I could not move. I tried to shake the blood from my forehead to at least see what was befalling me. A pile of wood and old furniture was being assembled in the middle of the Van Tassel front yard. I could feel myself shaking as I looked around for a friendly face in the crowd. Someone, anyone, who might be willing to offer me assistance, but I found none, even amongst the children who stared at the whole proceeding from behind their mothers' skirts. My eyes found Katrina, and she smiled coldly at me. "You might have saved yourself so much suffering, Ichabod Crane," she said as several men grabbed the ladder with my prostrate form and hauled it to the makeshift pyre, tossing me gracelessly atop of it. My limbs ached and throbbed; I was sure at least one of my left wrist bones was broken.

"The magic that protects Sleepy Hollow demands a blood sacrifice!" Katrina said, her voice rising above the din. "It was denied that sacrifice last year, and, good friends and neighbors, we all suffered for it. But now we may right the wrongs of this past year by spilling the blood that was meant to bless us!"

A cheer rose from the crowd. Several torches were lifted into my vision, and I knew I was white as a ghost, watching their flames sputter and dance. I could not move, only lie atop the pile of kindling, staring above me at the dark sky dotted with endless lines of diamond stars. The first torch was touched to the base, and I heard the crackling of dry wood catching. Several torches flew, landing next to me, one so precariously close to my arm that I could feel its flames licking at my shirtsleeve, threatening to consume it for the meat underneath.

The scream of an angry horse and the thunder of hooves sounded through the night, followed by screams, and a crash. I felt the earth suddenly shift from atop my funeral pyre, and I dropped, the ladder hitting the earth with a thud that made every bone in my body ache. The horse roared again, and I heard the hard, wet thump of steel meeting flesh. Chaos was all around me, a foot catching me in the jaw and knocking me senseless.

Familiar, black boots hit the dirt in front of me, and Reiter was there, pulling a knife from his belt and slicing the ropes that bound me to the ladder. I cried out when my broken wrist came free, and I saw his shoulders stiffen with rage. People were scattering around us, and I could see several figures sprawled upon the ground, though what their condition was, I did not know.

I could see fire starting to lick its way across the grass from where it had been scattered by the pyre's destruction. Reiter scooped me up and leaped upon Daredevil's back, holding me to his chest in front of him on the saddle as he gave the horse a kick, and Daredevil sprinted for the woods, scattering villagers left and right in his wake.

Reiter's head on the pommel addressed me as the hooves carried us further from the Van Tassel farm. "Are you all right, Ichabod?"

"I'll be fine," I groaned.

"The skull was not there," Reiter said, slowing Daredevil a bit as we plunged into the dark foliage of the forest. "I searched the entire cellar, but I could not find it."

My heart felt heavy in my chest at the words. Our mission was a failure. Reiter had saved me from a fiery death, but in only a few short hours, the last of my soul would be drained from my body by Katrina's magic, and I would be dead, leaving him alone once more. "I'm so sorry, Ichabod," he said, holding me close.

I gazed down into his face, studying every line of it. I lifted his head up with my hands, placing a gentle kiss on it. I felt tears on my cheeks, though I did not know if they came from me or him. As we pulled back, my eye caught something. The slightly twisted front tooth of his, and my brain snapped together with renewed vigor. "I know where your skull is!" I gasped.

He stared at me in confusion. "What?"

"It is on the mantle," I replied firmly. "I saw it before they dragged me out. We have to go back!"

"You're not safe there," Reiter said.

"I'm going to die soon if we don't kill Katrina," I said. "Please. We have to try."

Reiter hesitated, then nodded his assent. I kissed him again firmly before placing him back on the pommel, and he wheeled Daredevil around to charge back through the dark forest toward the Van Tassel estate.

We could hear the crowd before we could see it. One of the burning pieces from the pile had caught the barn, full of hay and feed, and it was a blazing inferno now. I saw the horses and cows and other animals gathered around the field as we approached, and villagers were tossing bucket after bucket of water onto the ground between the barn and the house to try to prevent the flames from spreading to the manor. I looked around for Katrina or Brom, but I could not see them in the chaos. The smoke was thick, and my throat and lungs already burned as we reached the edge of the trees.

"I am going in there with you," Reiter said as we approached the house, and I decided not to argue with him. I was in no shape to fight off anyone. He sprang down from Daredevil's back and helped me down before muttering something to the horse and then giving his flank a light smack. Daredevil whinnied, and then he was charging into the crowd of villagers, scattering them like ninepins.

Reiter and I dashed through the main door of the house and into the large parlor where the festivities had been occurring. The table still sat there, covered in all of its finery, though a few chairs and other things had been upended in the struggle to drag me outside earlier. I could see the skull still sitting on the mantlepiece amidst its decorations of sunflowers and tiny gourds. I raced for it, then stopped short as Baltus came at me out of the kitchen. He held a long, gleaming blade in his hand, and I realized that it was one of the swords that the American soldiers had used in their fights against English only a few years ago during the war. He swung it at me ferociously, obviously not skilled with it, but it still was plenty dangerous to drive me back and away from the mantle.

Reiter leaped in front of me, his knife out, and I heard the clash of steel as it met Baltus's sword. I lunged again for the fireplace, just as the monstrous gargoyle form of Brom Bones smashed through the front window and thundered toward me. Smoke poured in through the broken glass, immediately making my eyes water and sting. I braced myself as his bulk slammed into me, and I went flying into the chairs that were lining the room. My back slammed into the stone wall, driving the air from my lungs in a gasp, my body aching in pain. Brom's drooling mouth dipped and clamped onto the bicep of my right arm, stone fangs sinking deep into the muscle. I screamed as the agony flooded me.

Reiter's body turned to look at me, and Baltus plunged the sword into Reiter's chest, all the way to the hilt. I think I screamed again as Reiter staggered a step backward, my vision going blurry from Brom's jaws around me. Reiter reached up and yanked the sword from his chest, flipping it deftly in his grip before lunging and slashing across Baltus's throat. The old man's head tipped back, not completely severed from his body, but blood sprayed across the fancy linens and sumptuous feast. He dropped to his knees, catching the tablecloth as he did. Platters and delicacies tumbled to the ground around him as he fell upon his face and lay still in a spreading puddle of dark red blood.

With a snarl, Brom leaped at Reiter, taking him to the ground. The two scuffled, and I heard the clatter of something metallic. Through my blurred vision and the legs of the bench in front of me, I saw Reiter's dagger on the ground as he grappled with Brom. I heard the crunch of bone and saw Brom's jaw close around Reiter's ribs. Acting on pure adrenaline, I scrambled over the bench, my hands slick with blood. I caught the knife in my right hand and stabbed it at Brom's unprotected side. The blade glanced off of his stone hide, and he whirled on me, red eyes glowing, fangs bared in a crimson-tinged snarl.

Reiter shoved his gloved hands into Brom's mouth, behind his fangs, and yanked in opposite directions. Brom gurgled and howled, kicking and thrashing, dragging Reiter around the floor, but the Horseman held firm to his locked position around Brom's jaw. I looked to see if I could do anything to help, but the smoke was so thick inside now that I was struggling to breathe. I ran for the mantle and snatched up the skull from atop it. It felt lighter than I expected, with only the bones to it, and I turned back again just as Reiter put a burst of supernatural strength into his arms and ripped the lower jaw almost completely off of the gargoyle. Brom screamed, flopping about on the floor. Reiter pushed to his knees, grabbed the sword from where it had fallen, and plunged it straight down into the roof of Brom's gaping mouth. The creature went completely still, and then crumbled to dust at his feet.

I tried to call out to him, but I started coughing as the smoke permeated the room. I could hear crackling and feel heat nearby. I was sure the flames had spread to the house now. My eyes stung so much I couldn't even see, and I groped blindly around for anything at all.

Reiter's arms went around me, his jacket pulled up and over my head, and he quickly led me through the kitchen door. I felt an immediate temperature change when we stepped outside into the cool night. He kept me moving as I coughed and choked until we were some distance from the house, before he laid me on the grass. I sucked in deep lungfuls of night air, swiping at my face with a blood-soaked arm. Reiter hovered over me, his hands examining my wounds. I felt something sharp against my finger, and I realized I was still clutching the skull I had grabbed from the mantle. I held it out to him, still coughing, my eyes stinging.

He reached for it, but something struck him in the back, and his cloak ignited with flame. He reeled off of me, rolling across the grass, and I lifted my head to see Katrina standing nearby. Her blond hair was pulling wildly free from her braid, and her dress was smudged with soot and ash and blood. She opened her mouth to screech, revealing rows of razor-sharp pointed teeth. I saw her collect a ball of flame in her hand, and I braced myself for another fiery ending. She threw the fireball, but not at me as I expected. Instead, it struck the skull I dropped when Reiter had rolled off of me, and the entire thing exploded in a shower of orange flame.

Icy cold fear gripped me as I watched Reiter suddenly go completely limp on the ground, more still than I had ever seen him before. "No!" I knew he was gone before the strangled gasp even left my mouth. I crawled over to him, placing my hand on his chest, as if I expected to feel a heartbeat where there never had been one anyway. Anguish rocked through me, more painful than anything Katrina's magic had done, until my entire body was melting in agony hotter than the flames that burned behind me.

"Goodbye, Ichabod Crane," I heard Katrina say behind me. "I curse the day you came to Sleepy Hollow."

The scream that came out of me was more animal than man, made of rage and fury and absolute blinding hate. I snatched up the sword that had fallen from Reiter's grip. In one motion, I got to my feet, clutching the sword in both hands, and swung it with all of my might. The blade went through her neck and spine, and both Katrina's head and the blade flew across the air to land in the grass a dozen feet or more away. Her fingers that had morphed into the sickle-like blades retracted, and then her whole body began to shrivel and shrink. Her knees crumpled, and all of the color and moisture left her body. Before my very eyes, she withered and decayed until all that was left were her headless, mummified remains, sprawled on the ground, drowning in the fabric of her spoiled party dress.

Something crashed over me, and my body surged upward like I was breaking the surface of a massive wave. I inhaled sharply, feeling the pulse like the boom of a cannon ripple through me, over the burning Van Tassel farm, through the woods, over the village of Sleepy Hollow, and out to the river. I collapsed to the grass again, my whole body feeling like I had been splashed with icy water. I gasped and stared up at the stars winking above me, unchanged, even as the dark magic vanished from the glen.

I heard a sound next to me, no more than a soft rustle of fabric, and I turned to look where Reiter still lay at my side. He was curled on the ground like a newborn babe, his back to me. Every movement hurt me like the very devil was grinding my bones, but I forced myself to sit up. I saw movement from his chest that I had never seen before, and a strangled gasp left my throat when I realized it was breathing. I touched his arm, then drew back as he moaned and sat up.

And then, there he was, no longer head detached from body, but whole and complete like any other man. He turned to look at me, and despite the fact that he now looked as human as I, I was so used to seeing him as a headless specter that it was actually a shock to my system. His handsomely featured face, the one I had held cradled in my arms so many times, whose lips I had kissed, hair I had stroked, sat atop his shoulders and his repaired neck. His hand slid up to grasp at his throat, feeling where his body reattached, and he stared at me with a stunned expression that I was sure mirrored my own.

He was beautiful. I had always known it, but now, I could actually appreciate his appearance as a full man, and it was like seeing him for the first time. My breath caught in my throat as I stared into his dark eyes, and he into my green ones.

I was not sure who moved first, but we both lunged for one another, my hands catching around the back of his neck, his hands grasping my face, and our lips crashed together in a desperate, needy kiss that sent flames hotter than those of the Van Tassel's manor down my spine. His forehead pressed to mine, the tangled whisps of his dark hair brushing over my cheeks. "You did it," he whispered as he held me so close. "You really did it."

"*We* did it," I corrected him, and he kissed me firmly again.

A horse whinnied nearby, and Daredevil came around the side of the burning Van Tassel house, trotting over to us and stopping to sniffle and nuzzle Reiter's hair. He reached up to stroke the horse's nose. "Thank you, my friend," he said, and Daredevil chuffed into his hand.

Reiter pulled at my clothing to see my injuries. The wound on my arm from Brom had miraculously stopped bleeding and looked to almost be healed already; I noticed that where Brom had bitten Reiter's torso seemed now to be no more than ragged holes in his clothing as well. Reiter got to his feet and carefully helped me to mine. "I must ask one more favor of you," he said to Daredevil, and the horse grunted. He lifted me onto Daredevil's broad back, then followed me up, holding me close. "We must get you to a doctor in Tarry Town."

"I am all right," I tried to reassure him, though the shaking in my voice said otherwise. He gave me a kiss, then clucked to Daredevil, and the horse began to briskly trot around the house toward the forest path. The house was blazing, entirely consumed by flame now. With a crack and a shower of embers, it collapsed to the ground in a pile of ash and stone. A few people were standing dazedly about, watching the deadly blaze, and they lifted their eyes to us as we passed but did not move. One was Ezra Brouwer. Another was the Von Brussetts. All stared silently after us as Daredevil picked up his speed and began to canter through the forest path.

We encountered nearly every Sleepy Hollow family along the way, and not one of them accosted us, standing to the side to let us pass, no words exchanged. I could not bring myself to care about their plight right now. My whole body was wracked with pain, but that was overpowered by the incredible warmth from having Reiter at my back, steering Daredevil expertly along the dark road. We reached the fork, and, without so much as a pause, Daredevil took the fork to the right, toward the village. I turned my head just a bit to look at Reiter. "We are not going back to the church?"

"What for?" he asked. "I have the only thing I need, right here." And he kissed me again, soft and sweet, as we galloped through the glen of Sleepy Hollow.

The ride to Tarry Town was torture for my aching body, but Reiter's arms were firm around me, and Daredevil ran as smoothly as if the wind carried him. As we broke through the trees and onto the path up to the town, I could see the sentries at the closed gates. Reiter lifted a hand to them as we approached. "A doctor, please! We need a doctor!"

The sentries hurried to open the gate, and Daredevil dashed through them. One of the men directed us toward the doctor's quarters a few streets away, and the mustached man opened the door, still dressed in his nightgown and cap. Reiter jumped down from the horse and lifted me into his strong arms. The doctor ushered us into the surgery, and his wife met us there with candles and blankets.

The doctor set to work mending my body, from my broken wrist and sprained ankle to the burns and bruises that marred my skin. When asked if he was injured, Reiter said no, which seemed to be true. Other than his clothing sporting holes and rips from where he had battled the Van Tassels, he seemed to be entirely unblemished. He explained that there had been a fire at the Van Tassel estate, and the doctor seemed satisfied that my injuries had occurred from trying to help save the house and its inhabitants. "Were there any others injured?" the doctor asked as he tightly set my wrist. "Should we expect more people from the hollow?"

"I do not know," Reiter said. "If so, I think it will be morning before they make their way here."

The doctor nodded, then squinted at him through his spectacles. "I'm sorry, sir, I know who this fellow is, but I do not believe I got your name."

His warm hand slipped into mine and held it tight as he responded, "Reiter. Crane Reiter."

Epilogue

Reiter

It was several weeks before Ichabod had recovered enough for us to be able to travel, and by then, winter had set in, forcing us to remain where we were in Tarry Town. The townsfolk were very generous and provided us with supplies to let us stay in the schoolhouse, and we helped farmers clear snow and take care of their animals in exchange for meals.

Some of the villagers from Sleepy Hollow did make their way to Tarry Town in the days following the fire. I worried that perhaps they would recognize myself or Ichabod, but if they did, they made no mention or gesture toward either of us. They did have quite the remarkable tale to tell about a Headless Horseman who would take heads on Halloween night though, and, many years later, this story was still being circulated as local folklore. I paid it no mind. If it brought them comfort to blame the Horseman now that the curse had been lifted, what point would there be in contradicting it?

The memories of my life before I had been cursed, along with my name, never returned. Ichabod offered to help me search the area records for people who might potentially have been my family and see if my name was recorded anywhere, but I told him no. While I appreciated that he wanted to give me some closure to the life I could not remember, it was so long ago that it was unlikely that it would mean that much to me even if we did find that information. I had been the Headless Horseman for a century, and now I was Crane Reiter. Ichabod was my family and my future. My past was behind me, as it was behind him.

It was strange to be back in my full body after so long, and more than once I forgot how tall I was when I cracked my head on a doorframe or underneath the table when retrieving something I dropped. The first time we shared intimacies with one another after he had regained his strength, Ichabod teased me that he might miss all of the amazing things I could do with my head separated from my body, and I vowed to him I would be as creative as possible to give him even more pleasure in my restored form. But we both agreed that being able to kiss and embrace, face to face, arms around one another, made up for any deficiencies caused by my lack of flexibility.

After the winter passed, Ichabod and I discussed what we wanted to do. There were many options to consider. We could find a quiet place to settle down. He could resume his travels as a schoolmaster, with me to accompany him. We could return to Connecticut, to the place where he grew up. We made a visit to New York City, but both of us determined that city life was much too busy for us, while country farming life was too quiet and caused us both distress at times. So, we traveled. Up and down the Hudson, from town to town, state to state, for many years.

When next I heard of Sleepy Hollow, after we had been away from New York for a number of years, I heard that the population of the area had grown to more than triple what it had been when we left it, and it was continuing to thrive. I had no desire to revisit the town to see it for myself, but the knowledge that it too had moved on from the Van Tassel curse was a balm to my spirit.

Time has passed, and Ichabod and I have moved with it. The years feel shorter now, but every moment is precious to us, for we know that our life on this earth is limited. I do not regret my years spent in purgatory, for without them, I would never have found him. So, I continue to smile whenever I hear a recounting of the story of the Headless Horseman of Sleepy Hollow, whatever iteration it may be, for I know the truth, and the truth is better than any ghost story.

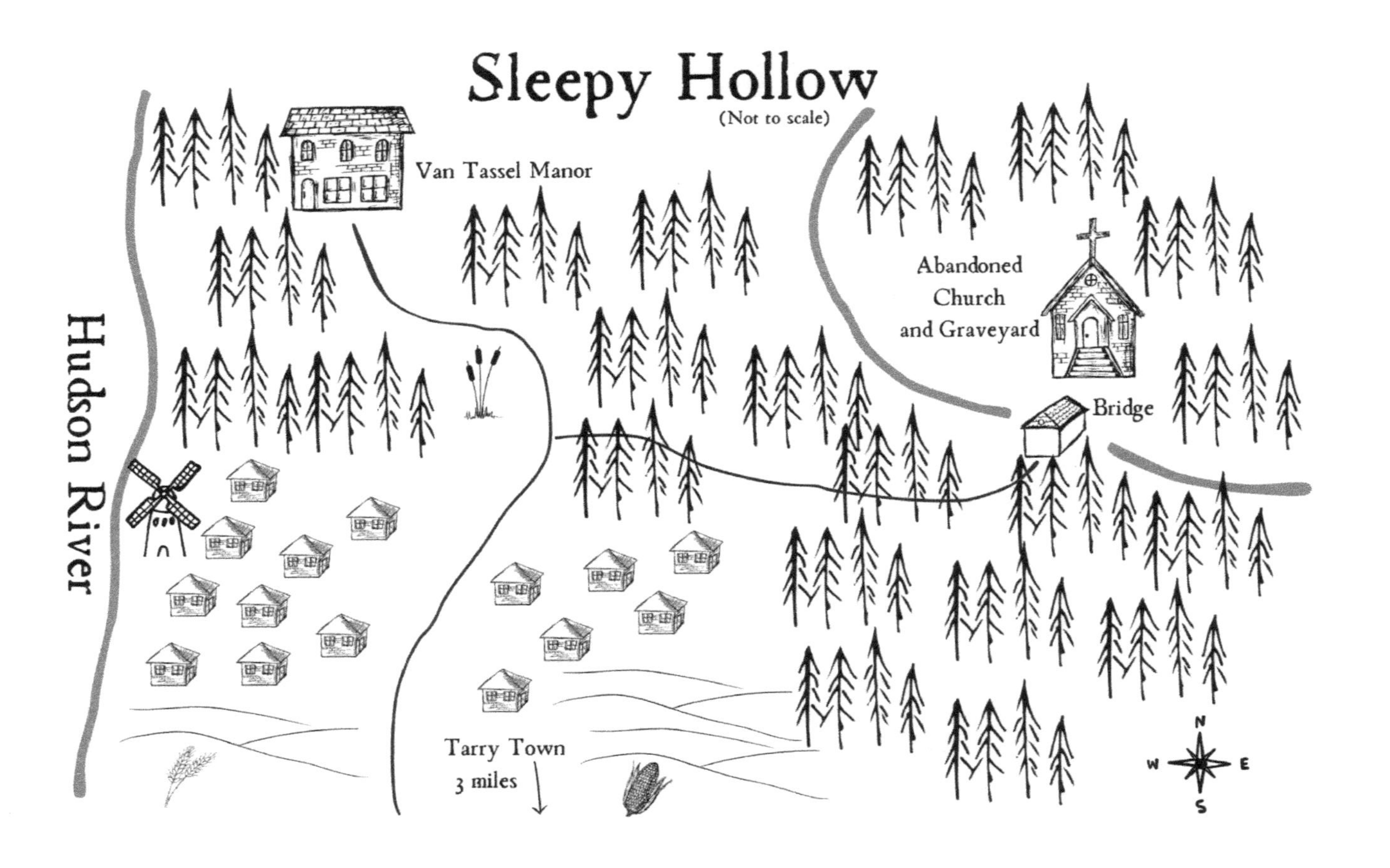
Sleepy Hollow
(Not to scale)
Van Tassel Manor
Abandoned
Church
and Graveyard
Bridge
Hudson River
Tarry Town
3 miles
N
W
E
S

About the Author

Kit Barrie (she/her) was raised by pirates in a traveling carnival where she learned how to fly and to weave fantasy into reality. She identifies as chaotic bisexual, with good intentions and questionable methods. She lives in an utterly unfantastical state in the Midwestern United States with her very supportive spouse (VSS) and at least 4 food goblins who might just be cats gobblin' food.

Please visit www.kitbarrie.com or scan the QR code below for more information on Kit and her other available titles.

Printed in the USA
CPSIA information can be obtained
at www.ICGtesting.com
JSHW020722021023
49212JS00001B/22